MISS ISABELLE'S CRAVING

The Search Duology
Book 2

Imogene Nix

Print ISBN 978-1-922369-02-4

Foreword

Miss Isabelle's Craving is the sequel to Miss Elspeth's Desire. It's been written well over 12 months after the first instalment and concludes the series—which began rather like a bet against myself that I could not just write an Historical romance, but also do it well.

Having said that, when I sat down to begin I considered what era of time and the countries I loved… India has always intrigued me but China is one of those countries that calls to you on an instinctive level. As a result, it made a lot of sense to base the second book in Shanghai and give Isabelle a totally different backdrop for her book. After all, she's been patient and deserves to stand out.

Shanghai during this time was annexed by some countries, those looking for a toehold in China. This is where I began, hence the English settlement I used. There were indeed banks (and yes, The Oriental Bank was based in Shanghai and carried out a lot of business with the English who lived there.) In fact, many of the sites I've used did and continue to exist.

I always feel that the mid to late Victorian times are the forgotten era (particularly the later Victorian 1870+) which is a shame as it was an age of invention and change and dramatic social revolution. It was also a time of unrest with the Boxer Rebellion, politic tension between the Chinese Empire and the British Government and so much more. It also was truly the time of "Opium Eaters," who were addicts in the greatest sense of the word.

I have taken lengths to ensure my facts concerning Shanghai in particular in this title are correct. There was so much to learn! The importation of opium was an issue and used to control the populace, as was ownership of land in the region, the concessions and even the telegraph and railway lines.

For those who note the spelling of the *Yang-tzu Chiang* yes it was an earlier name for the *Yangtze River*. The name is the anglicisation of the name based on the Beijing dialect and was in use until 1906.

The Shanghai Municipal Council controlled the police (though I may have taken a few liberties so Langdon could take up a role there.) The Shanghai Municipal Police were formed in September of 1854 and were dissolved on 31 July 1943, and their role was the jurisdiction of the Shanghai International Settlement.

Where there may be inaccuracies, I beg for forgiveness and forbearance of the reader, and I thank you for sharing this journey with me.

Dedicated to my family, my readers and most of all, my husband.

Imogene Nix
2020

Chapter One

ISABELLE'S HAND hovered over her journal page, the fountain pen—a relatively new invention—sitting just above the heavy paper.

January 1879
It's been difficult since my illness in Calcutta and Bombay. I
have had so few opportunities to write openly about the time since
we left England. Even though we are now bound for Shanghai,
and quite close according to the captain, my excitement is
dimmed. I fear my illness returning, and though I have Jacinthe
here, the thought of any further debilitation fills me with dread.
I find the long hours of this voyage taxing—the hours without
actual occupation tedious. Without much to do, I read and draw,
yet I yearn for something to capture my attention. A way to fill
my mind, so I may rest easy.
In the darkness of night, I also find myself fearing the sounds I
sometimes hear emanating from the cabin next to me. The one
Aeddan and Elspeth share.
They do try to be quiet, but sometimes, I cannot help but hear. I
am not unaware of the hungers of the flesh.

The pen rose as Isabelle looked toward the open

window. It wasn't easy to pour out the myriad of fears that filled her mind.

When I was younger, I'd listen to the housemaids' chatter. It didn't seem to be pleasurable then with the talk of heat and fury, but now I hear Elspeth, and I wonder at the glow I see on her face. The joy that radiates from her daily.

I am genuinely pleased for my sister, but for myself, there is nothing but despair.

Perhaps it is the knowledge that Louisa is married and expecting her first child and Elspeth is happy with her choice.

Truly, Aeddan is a perfect foil for Elspeth, and the jealousy I feel sickens me. He is good. Attentive and kind. Resourceful and loving. Everything she deserves.

In my future, I see nothing similar.

No possibility of the pleasure I cannot sometimes escape the echoes of. What if that is all that exists? A spinsterhood that stretches into the future? It's not enough.

I should learn to be content.

I will strive tomorrow to be more. To find an inner well of self-containment, but I fear this is not a skill I possess.

I

Scrubbing at her eyes, Isabelle sighed, blew softly on the page then sanded it so the ink wouldn't bleed, before closing the leather cover of her diary. Jacinthe snored lightly in the bunk on the other side of the cabin as the vessel swayed gently.

Isabelle reached over and placed the diary on the trunk beside her bed and turned the knob, extinguishing the lamp. She lay down, gaze settled on the horizon, the blanket pulled closer against the cold breeze. Moonlight filtered in through the open window, and she lay there a long time contemplating it before finally giving in to slumber.

*A*eddan sat at the head of the table, the captain taking the opposite position. "We are perhaps five days from Shanghai, and we shall see some vessels soon."

Isabelle sipped her tea. "I have heard that there are two separate townships that make up Shanghai, Captain. Is that correct?"

The grizzled man glanced at her. "Indeed, there are more than two, Miss Isabelle. The Chinese and Europeans do not inhabit the same areas, but they are called *concessions*. The territories are English and French to name a few. The Chinese are forbidden from owning property in the concessions, though I've heard tell that some have begun leasing properties on the waterfront."

"Why is that, Captain?" enquired Elspeth, fanning herself. Her sister did look slightly unwell and ate little. Isabelle also noted the way Aeddan paid extra attention to her sister. Perhaps she'd enquire later if she were unwell, she thought, then turned her attention back to the discussion.

"Spite in terms of plain talking, Miss Isabelle. Since the Shanghai municipal council has taken over the running of the majority of the European section, the Chinese officials have demanded we curb what we do. Why they even caused issues with both the telegraph and rail line. The result is the rail has since shut and is now removed. A bad business indeed."

Isabelle couldn't hide her interest. "Telegraph? You mean there would be communication? Excellent." For the first time in a long while, Isabelle looked forward to landfall. Perhaps in this exotic locale, she'd find something to fulfill her in the years ahead.

Chapter Two

STARING through the window at the rear of the ship, Isabelle savored the sounds and scents of this new land. Unlike their mooring in India, this time she was well, though Elspeth still attempted to mollycoddle her.

In the last few days, they'd seen all manner of transport ships, carrying exotic items to the many corners of the world, the sails an unusual size and shape, and she'd enquired of the captain as to their efficacy. Now they'd docked, and the time had come to explore a new port. Indeed, she'd already had more than a full day and night to watch the movements from the deck, Aeddan having requested they wait to leave the ship until he could find suitable accommodations.

"Are you coming, dearest?" Elspeth called to her through the door of the cabin as Isabelle tied the strings of her bonnet.

"Of course, Elspeth." She gathered her gloves and reticule, the ivory handle of her parasol swinging from an artfully carved crook which draped over her arm.

Jacinthe would follow, Elspeth assured her, with a sailor or two to attend to the transportation of their trunks, but they'd go ahead. Their man of business had already secured accommodation for them in the British concession.

Excitement fizzed in Isabelle's veins as she climbed up the ladder and crossed the deck. She inhaled deeply, letting the unfamiliar fragrances fill her senses, along with the sounds of voices speaking in a range of lyrical cadences and languages.

The noise of people milling, animals waiting on the dock, and boxes banging and crashing captured her attention. The din of voices filling the air as she made her way down the gangplank gave her pause for a moment, then she smiled, barely noting the jouncing movement of the gangway beneath her feet.

"Aeddan said he'd been here before," Elspeth assured her at the bottom, and Isabelle merely nodded as she gazed at the vista before her.

"It's so different." It truly was. The landscape felt both familiar and yet so alien. The faces of the locals strange to her gaze. Skin tones of burnished copper, some with more yellow tints. Swarthy Mediterranean men and rosy burnt white Englishmen were numerous in the workers before her.

"Aeddan has arranged a carriage to meet us. He sent Grundy to escort us."

Grundy was Aeddan's valet. A gnarled man in his fourth decade, though he looked older, with lines etched into his face and a spare frame. He and Aeddan had boarded the *Zephyr* in Bombay during Elspeth and Isabelle's voyage to India, and he was a trusted member of the household.

Isabelle almost remonstrated, then caught sight of Elspeth's face. "There's some reason we must have an escort?"

"He feels one cannot be too careful." They kept a brisk pace and headed to where the man waited for them by a battered conveyance.

Once handed into the cabin, they settled themselves as best they could, Grundy swinging up the front and giving directions, and they set off.

The sea of people parted for them, some watching with narrowed gazes and others with wistful looks. "We should send the *Jamestown* on ahead of us. Fill it with stock. It'll arrive in England and likely be back before we are ready to leave."

Elspeth opened her mouth then closed it again on a wince. "Elspeth?"

Her sister smoothed the gown over her lap. "When we are settled in our accommodation,

I feel we should talk." Elspeth's gaze moved over Isabelle's then slid away.

Isabelle narrowed her eyes but kept her counsel. She couldn't guess at what her sister was hiding, but it discommoded her. She and Elspeth had always been in total agreement over matters relating to Forster Shipping. Surely things weren't about to change now?

The commercial buildings they passed wore imposing façades. The white stone monoliths she quickly recognized as features of the colonies. Towering columns of white looking out with high arches, built to catch the breeze, she thought. Children ran along the side of the road, some dressed strangely, pants and top held together with ornate frog closures, their hair a glossy black. Others wore the ragged look of street urchins, with grimy faces. Here and there they passed well- groomed children, accompanied by women in western clothing—probably nannies, thought Isabelle.

India had indeed been eye-opening, but she'd been too ill in the beginning to take it in properly with malaria sapping her strength. The time she'd spent with Lady Manton had been insightful, socially. She'd been encouraged to participate in social banter and form friendships with other young women, though most had been married and had established families. Isabelle wasn't unaware that men watched her. Her trim figure, blonde hair, and blue eyes would always intrigue men, but very few sought what she did—a soul-deep connection. The kind she saw between her sister Elspeth and Aeddan.

Louisa had settled for a simple relationship and the safety

of a younger son. She and Jeremy—now wed a year—had taken residence in the family home, and Louisa, the soft female that she was, would forever feel cosseted and safe.

Elspeth and Aeddan, on the other hand, had sought adventure and passion in India. On their return, the couple would likely set up home in London.

The sad truth was, Isabelle had made no plans for her future, now that the original ones— those she and Elspeth had made before setting sail aboard the *Zephyr* for India—were to be set aside.

Turning forward once more, Isabelle spied a house through the glass. Not some distance away, she noted another settlement, and when she enquired, Isabelle was informed that it was the French section as Grundy called it. Beyond that, he said, lay the Chinese settlement which foreigners weren't welcomed to visit.

The conveyance pulled to a halt beside a high-walled property. It was imposing with ornate wrought iron gates. The gates slid inwardly, pulled by two large ropes. The horses neighed as they entered the driveway, the hooves and wheels crunching on the long, full drive before stopping at a portico.

The carriage swayed as they alighted, and the two women were ushered inside.

"Madam. Miss. I'm the housekeeper, Mrs. Hargraves." The female servant, portly but carefully dressed and aged in her fourth or fifth decade, bobbed a tiny curtsey and guided them up the wide staircase. "I've taken the liberty of preparing your chambers. Mr. Fitzsimmons was most emphatic that you were both to have time to rest before the dinner hour, and he asked me to tell you he'd be back before then."

The woman stopped at a set of magnificent dark wood doors and slid them open to reveal a bedchamber decorated in pale floral tones. "Madam, Mr. Fitzsimmons said this was to be your chamber, and Miss Isabelle is to have one down the hall."

With a glance at Elspeth, Isabelle followed the woman down to a chamber at the end. The room was almost as large and decorated in pale greens and gold accents. Pretty enough but the colors not to her taste. *I won't tell anyone that though.*

"I'll have the girls bring up water for you so you can bathe. Then perhaps a rest?" the woman added hopefully.

"Once my trunks have arrived, I would appreciate them being unpacked. I have some things to attend to, and Mr. Staindhouse of Forster Shipping will be here shortly to meet with me." Isabelle tugged off her gloves and smiled at the woman. "If there is a small parlor I might use for private meetings? I'll require paper and ink and tea."

The housekeeper appeared shocked. "You'll be meeting him alone?"

Oh dear. This is not like home. The running of Forster Shipping had been shared between the two women for years, ever since their father's passing, but at home, people understood they were women of business. Here, the rules were changed on them. Even in India, she'd had restrictions placed on her meetings with their man in Calcutta.

"Jacinthe will attend me when she arrives. She's my sister's maid, but for propriety, you understand?"

Mrs. Hargraves peered at her nervously. "Of course. You'll be wishing to engage your own maid though?"

"Perhaps," Isabelle hedged and entered the room. "Send the water along and Jacinthe after she's attended my sister. Thank you."

*T*he woman stepped back, and the doors closed behind her.

Major Langdon Amberton Deveraux knocked back the

liquor in his glass, then thudded it down onto the bar. "Well, my friend, it seems I'm at a loose end. Left to attend all those society rounds alone, now that you've made your announcement."

Justin, his confidante and comrade-in-arms, had just relayed the news of his impending nuptials. "We'll be heading to England as soon as we're wed. The family demands to meet her and all."

Langdon could take offense at the information, but why would he? It wasn't that Langdon didn't like the fiancée. All to the opposite. He'd enjoyed her company very well, long before Justin had laid eyes on her. They'd met at balls and the tea parties he'd not been able to avoid. Not that he'd personally squired her, though for a short while, Langdon had even considered making a play for the young lady in question, but Amelia Watchope—of the correct breeding and social status —was now beyond his grasp. Unsurprisingly, he felt no real remorse at the loss of her presence.

"But you'll attend. Stand up for me?" Justin appeared very young in that moment, with a lock of sandy hair obscuring his view. He flopped it out of the way, his earnest blue eyes imploring Langdon.

Justin had shown immense promise in the realms of diplomacy, and Amelia would enhance that. He had no doubt. "Of course I shall." Langdon rose and clapped the man on the back. "Congratulations. Now, I must be off. I'm to meet this fellow, Fitzsimmons."

He retreated outside and jammed his hat onto his head. Fitzsimmons was ostensibly here with his wife and sister-in-law who were somehow affiliated with Forster Shipping, though why they'd come to Shanghai at this time was strange. The walk back was bracing as his mind turned to the matter at hand.

His role right now was to work with the municipal council. There were issues, and he'd been directed by the acting consul general to assist as necessary. If he happened to come across dealings which caused concern to the government, well that was lucky indeed.

He stepped inside the Shanghai municipal council office and had barely filled his seat when the door opened and in strode a forceful-looking man. One he knew slightly. Aeddan Fitzsimmons. A major in the queen's forces and a distant relative if he remembered his family connections right.

"Fitzsimmons?"

"Langdon." Fitzsimmons nodded and held out his hand. They shook.

Langdon took a moment to size the other man up. Tall, with a muscular physique. Dark hair and gray eyes. Yes, he looked like many of the Fitzsimmons men of Langdon's acquaintance.

Now, Langdon proceeded to the door and shut it. He motioned to Aeddan to take a seat. "Tell me, how can I assist you?"

*H*aving taken the time to bathe and dress in a fresh gown, Isabelle made her way to the parlor Mrs. Hargraves had indicated she'd prepared for her use. As she passed the clock in the hall, she took notice of the time. Almost two in the afternoon. Surely Staindhouse would attend her shortly? The Forster women had always appreciated the timeliness of their retainers.

Her arm shook; the massive ledger she carried contained a list of the items they'd sourced from the region previously, and the weight of it left her arms aching.

The result of my illness.

Modern medicine had offered her relief, and she'd be forever grateful to the doctor who'd attended her aboard the

Zephyr in Bombay. Without the quinine... The thought nipped at her as it always did.

Settling herself in the chair she'd chosen, Isabelle opened the tome and perused it. Tea. Jade. Medicinal items.

The last item left her wondering what exactly that included. Their man at home had declared them to be herbal medications likely, but the answer had never satisfied Isabelle completely. She'd heard of opium and indeed had partaken of laudanum as and when required by her physician, though only ever in minuscule doses. What she couldn't countenance though was those who partook for recreational reasons. Even the term 'opium-eater' made her stomach clench with anger, but she released it to the heavens, more than aware that some people lacked any sort of willpower to overcome such addictions.

A knock echoed on the door. "Enter," she called, and a small man entered the room, Mrs. Hargraves hovering in the doorway. "Please bring tea through in twenty minutes. We should be ready by then."

Mrs. Hargraves's eyes strayed to Jacinthe, where she sat in the corner of the room, hands employed stitching a handker-chief. Isabelle watched Mrs. Hargraves until the door closed behind her.

The man bowed deeply and dropped into the chair she indicated.

"Staindhouse? You've worked for Forster Shipping for three years here in Shanghai, is that correct?"

He held his hat in nervous, twitching hands. "Yes, Miss Forster."

"And before that you were employed by one of the mercantiles in Shanghai for nearly ten years. Correct? You've managed to acquire a range of suppliers for tea, jade, and medicinal products. Can you tell me what products they may be?"

His mouth dropped. "It's um...herbal substances. Plants and things."

"And none of them are enhanced with opium?"

He shook his head, alarm spreading over his face as he blanched. "No, Miss. Your captains made it clear you'd not allow opium aboard on account of your concerns about opium- eaters and the crew. As you know, the trade is more from India to China, rather than the other way around."

The pit which had yawed in her belly subsided. So, the medicinal items, as described, should be acceptable. Of course, there'd need to be further investigation so she knew what the mixture contained, but she could be assured the man sitting opposite her was not involved in smuggling the produce of the poppy. She'd previously received worrying intelligence that from time to time their shipments had been tainted with the product, and she was determined to stamp that out.

"I'd like to increase our Chinese tea imports in the next year—green and black both. Also, there is an interest in Chinese antiquities—porcelains and so on. I'd like you to investigate those options for me and report back with all due speed. Jade is still popular as are Chinese silks. We've already found new suppliers of Indian materials, but I'd like to increase our wares. We are dealing with reputable people, yes?"

Staindhouse nodded. "Yes, Miss. I'm planning on heading out soon to make an audit of our suppliers."

Isabelle cocked her head. "Truly? I'd be interested in joining you."

His lips took on a pinched appearance. "If I may be so bold, Miss Forster. That would be unwise. Unaccompanied ladies are considered brazen and loose. Perhaps Mr. Fitzsimmons would be—"

Isabelle twitched her gloves, unhappy with the answer. "Alas, he is not in a position to undertake such tasks for myself or my sister. I'll make inquiries concerning a lady to—"

He shook his head, indicating his worry. "No, Miss. A gentleman is the only one they will deal with."

She released a breath. "A gentleman?" Isabelle clenched her fingers. "Then I shall look into this and apprise you of my plans once they are settled."

Mrs. Hargraves entered the room, bustling in with a large pot of tea, two cups, lemon, sugar, and milk. "Teatime, Miss Forster."

Once their drinks were poured, Isabelle steered the conversation to other, safer topics. Learned about his family, the other staff on her payroll locally, and issues they'd encountered doing business with the Chinese. Once Staindhouse rose and made his exit, Isabelle stood and paced the room. It was irksome that such male-dominated traditions would hamper her work, but alas, even in England some such barriers still existed.

While she considered the issue of a gentleman to accompany her, the door opened and her sister, Elspeth, slipped inside.

Fatigue emanated from her, and Isabelle frowned. "Come sit down, Elspeth."

Her sister dipped gratefully onto the chaise and faced her. "We should talk, dearest." Isabelle took up a position on her seat and waited for whatever was to come. Her sister

appeared wan and unsettled, fingers alternately clenching in her lap or picking at the lace decorating her gown.

"Isabelle, we cannot remain in Shanghai for long." The hesitancy in Elspeth's voice worried Isabelle, and she sat forward in her seat.

"Why?"

"Aeddan, as you know, is not just a Major. His role as his father's heir is undeniable, and the Earl is unwell and has been for some time. He's requested Aeddan and I to return immediately. He is needed to handle the estate and other family matters."

Isabelle frowned. "I understand that, but I could stay here. Take on a companion and—"

"No, Isabelle. There are other reasons." Now her sister averted her gaze, but Isabelle caught sight of the way she bit her lower lip. "I'm expecting, Isabelle. We must return to England, and Aeddan has warned me that you shouldn't be left here alone. He says the political situation—"

Shock hammered at Isabelle. "Expecting?"

Her sister turned back and gave a nod while perched on the edge of the seat. The wide- eyed look pleaded with Isabelle to understand, forgive, and accept. "Yes. We need to be in England by the time I give birth, and should his father not recover from his illness, Aeddan needs to be there. We can stay here in Shanghai but a month."

"But Shanghai..." The bottom fell out of Isabelle's world. "We've just arrived and—" "I am sorry, Isabelle. It's not what anyone planned."

*L*angdon followed Aeddan into the house on the edge of the British concession. It was large enough to be comfortable, with columns raising verandahs following the lines of the house, and cleverly designed to catch the breezes. The French section bounded nearby so there was traffic and movement enough that it was safely in the center of a well-utilized thoroughfare, yet quiet enough to offer serenity in the land area bounded by lush trees, though the winter frost currently denuded them. The area was bustling and well-to-do.

He and Fitzsimmons entered the hall and were met by a hovering maidservant. "Mrs. Fitzsimmons and Miss Forster are already in the salon, sir. May I take your hat and coat?"

They both surrendered them to the housekeeper and entered the room to the left of the foyer.

Langdon noted the furnishings of brocade in reds and gold. A seat facing the door and winged chairs with their backs to the door. The effect was traditional, and English as so many of these lease houses tended to be.

A woman—beautiful with shining titian locks—rose, her smile giving the appearance of a welcoming goddess, and she approached them. He caught the glint of gold on her hand and smiled, suddenly aware that this was Fitzsimmons's wife.

"Aeddan, you're just in time, and this must be Major Deveraux?" she said.

Langdon nodded and took the woman's hand. "Mrs. Fitzsimmons, it's an honor and a pleasure."

Fitzsimmons had explained his wife and sister-in-law would be waiting for them. Having posted ahead, they'd both be joining them for dinner. Langdon was thankful for the welcome. It wasn't always so with travelers to the region, particularly those engaged in any form of commerce lately. After all, his role with the municipal government was at best polarizing, and at worst, the stick minus a carrot. He was engaged in correcting any form of corruption within the organization as well as investigating other things of interest to the British government.

He bowed as appropriate, then stepped back.

A movement to his right caught his attention, and a vision of womanly perfection rose from a wing chair. Her hair silvery —white gold and shorter than fashion dictated—suited the peaches and cream skin tone. Her tresses framed a flawless visage which featured high cheekbones, a soft forehead, and piercing, sapphire blue eyes. Her svelte figure was narrow enough that his hands might span her waist.

The effect was of an elfin creature. Ethereal yet somehow human.

She smiled a welcome.

Mrs. Fitzsimmons nodded to the younger woman. "Major Deveraux, pray meet my sister, Miss Isabelle Forster."

The woman slid her fingers over his palm, and a shock of energy sizzled. She eyed him gravely as if expecting something unpleasant or unexpected to happen.

"Miss Forster. It's a delight." *Indeed, it's a pleasure.*

She cocked her head to one side. Their gazes clashed, eyes at the same level, he noted, taking in the height of this woman.

"The pleasure is mine, Major." Her manner was precise and correct, yet didn't invite anything more personal, so he retreated.

"Come, Mrs. Hargraves has organized refreshments while we await dinner," Mrs. Fitzsimmons's urged.

They each settled into a seat, and Langdon couldn't help the frisson of awareness as the woman returned to the sizeable winged chair which surrounded her. He accepted a drink, as did the others gathered around, and the chatter held a subdued quality.

When dinner was served, Fitzsimmons and his wife moved ahead, and Langdon offered his arm to Isabelle. She took it, her hand settling on his with a tiny quiver.

"You're very quiet, Miss Forster."

"I prefer to observe people first, Major. That allows me to form an opinion of their veracity."

He quirked a brow. "Really? That is important to you?" Langdon wondered how she'd answer.

She didn't so much as blink. "I have not yet formed a view where you are concerned, Major, though I have no doubt that will come. With time."

She marched into the dining room and settled herself at the table, the bronze and figured silver of her gown catching in the lamplight. The shining curl of her hair entranced him, and he made a mental note to learn more about this woman.

At first glance, she appeared young, but the way she spoke, and her confidence, assured him she was more mature than he'd initially thought. Perhaps two or three and twenty?

Dinner passed in a companionable fashion, with Fitzsimmons and his wife regaling Langdon with snippets of their journey through India.

"The elephant made this tremendous noise and startled the horse. I swear, I've never heard anything the like before or since," added Mrs. Fitzsimmons.

"Miss Forster traveled with you?"

The woman's face closed tight before his gaze; any openness she may have displayed earlier now withered away. "No, Major. I remained with Lady Manton and partook of the society instead." There was a touch of bitterness in her voice that he wondered at but kept his counsel.

When the ladies retired to the salon, he glanced at Fitzsimmons. "Miss Forster isn't one to enjoy an adventure?" The question was the only acceptable way he could ask what he wanted to know.

"She contracted malaria on the voyage to India after their maid perished in a storm. It was taxing for them both. While Isabelle was recovered, her reserves were low, so her sister and I agreed that she wasn't well enough to undertake the trip to the villages, and she remained behind."

Fitzsimmons's glare cut through him. The other man slid his glass to the table and pierced Langdon with a knowing gaze.

"She's my sister in every way that counts, Deveraux. I would hate for someone to trifle with her affections."

Langdon lifted his glass. "Point made, cousin."

They finished the excellent port then entered the salon, the two women busy at their tasks. Miss Isabelle was poring over a book that he thought looked suspiciously like a ledger, though she flipped it shut as they neared. Mrs. Fitzsimmons worked on an embroidery project, beside her a basket full of skeins in vibrant jeweled colors.

Miss Forster rose, captured their gaze, so they stilled. "Gentlemen, if you'll excuse me. The day has been trying—"

Langdon bowed deeply. "The hour grows late indeed, and you've just arrived, so I should bid you adieu." The party broke up, and he took his leave, retrieving his hat and coat at the door. The air settled around him, cold in the late winter month. He shivered as he climbed into a coach just beyond the gate and gave his direction with a slight smile. "I'll be back," he murmured to the night.

Isabelle rose early the next morning. If all she had was a month, then she'd need to be filling it with the tasks she'd planned to achieve.

The gown she slipped into—mint green with dark gray stripes—fit snugly. Maybe a little too much so, she thought. Not for the first time, Isabelle sighed at the folly of ordering new gowns in India after her bout of illness.

"I'll need to have them let out," she grumbled.

She settled at the small boudoir table to fashion her hair while she waited for assistance. Jacinthe slipped into the room and completed the task of fastening the gown, and she'd just slipped on her pelisse as Elspeth called for the maid.

"It's fine. Go to my sister, Jacinthe. I'll see Mrs. Hargraves about a maid to accompany me." Indeed, sharing Jacinthe hadn't been an issue previously, but with Elspeth increasing, maybe it was time to attend to her own needs?

She slipped the thought away to discuss with Mrs. Hargraves later in the day, and she'd ask about finding a dressmaker too, one able to alter or sew her new gowns. The old ones were sadly stained and ill-fitting since they'd left their home port.

Hurrying down the staircase, she stopped at the bottom and stared at the man inside the doorway, his arms filled with baskets.

"Missy want buns?" The man grinned at her, teeth wide as his head bobbed up and down.

Isabelle blinked and stepped back as Mrs. Hargraves shuffled forward from the kitchen, using the long hallway as her thoroughfare. "What did I tell you, Ah Ching? Out the back now, and don't bother Miss Forster." Then Mrs. Hargraves sent her a quick apology.

Before the woman could bustle off, Isabelle called, "Wait!"

The older lady turned. "Miss Isabelle?"

"Is there a maid who would be able to accompany me? I need to go to the office and meet with Mr. Staindhouse."

Mrs. Hargraves blinked. "There's Mei. She's young but... Just a moment, Miss Isabelle." The woman disappeared around the corner, arms flapping as she urged the local forward, and Isabelle waited, her gaze dropping to the salver by the door. Already there was a goodly number of cards and invitations. *Leave that to Elspeth.* No doubt they'd be engaged nightly soon enough.

Except, Isabelle didn't want to be 'engaged' in social pursuits as her sister now seemed to be.

It wasn't so much that Elspeth had foregone her interest in Forster Shipping, but the task of a household, husband, and now impending parenthood seemed to have swept away her time to focus on what needed to be attended to.

There were tasks to complete, cargo to order, books and ships to inspect. New markets to open. Isabelle was a woman of business and unashamed of that fact. Elspeth now had a titled husband, and Forster Shipping was always going to be secondary to this new existence.

Unlike her sister, Isabelle would continue her work long after their return to England, while Elspeth would have a family. Children. *Even if I did have a family, Forster Shipping is far too important. It's more than just our heritage. It's what we'd leave behind for future generations.* Not that she'd likely be adding to them, she thought, the bitter note ringing in her mind.

Isabelle shut down the instinctive ache. No good came from wishful thinking.

Instead, she considered what she'd learned aboard the *Jamestown*. Elspeth was now the Viscountess Traughton—not that either Aeddan or Elspeth used their substantive titles. They'd impressed on Isabelle the danger of doing so until they were safely on English soil again, away from those who wished to use the Forster Shipping Line for their own nefarious means.

If Isabelle could ferret out who was behind the threats, then perhaps she'd be able to return later on to Shanghai? Aeddan wouldn't appreciate the steps she'd take, but if she wanted freedom, there was no other choice. As much as she liked her new brother-in-law, she wouldn't allow him to investigate on her behalf. Forster Shipping was now her responsibility, and ignoring the danger was utterly incomprehensible.

"I'm a resourceful woman of means," Isabelle reminded herself as Mrs. Hargraves bustled back into the hallway, tugging a young woman of maybe eighteen behind her.

"This is Mei. I can spare her to you if you like."

The girl shot her an anxious look, and Isabelle sized her up. "She'll be perfect," she answered and beckoned the girl forward and out the door.

Mei's face took on an apprehensive slant. "Missy should not travel alone," she said quietly, and Isabelle glanced at the girl.

"Why not?"

The girl bowed her head, and her hands burrowed deep in her sleeves. "Only women of loose morals go in public without an escort."

Isabelle considered her words, the cadence of them, the shape of her eyes, and the color of her skin, and frowned. "You're not fully Chinese, are you?"

The girl shook her head, the black braids whipping to and

fro. "My father is English. My mother was a concubine he kept."

Isabelle's breath exhaled. "What?" The word exploded at an almost shriek.

Mei blanched. "Come, Miss. We should find a carriage." The girl moved forward on rapid feet as if it were safer to hail a cab than to answer questions. After flagging one down, she assisted Isabelle in and climbed in after her. "Where do we go?"

Isabelle gave the direction, which Mei promptly repeated to the driver, and with a jerk, they clattered off down the road.

In silence, Isabelle scanned the girl's face. *An Englishman keeping concubines?* How could that even happen? She knew exactly what they were, having spied more than one harem while in India. Several princes had regularly joined the society of the English and brought multiple senior wives with them. She'd met many with more than one foot in each world.

Concluding that remaining quiet was the best option for now, they traveled in silence, the rock of the carriage soothing her a little.

Chapter Three

LANGDON ROSE, aware that he'd rested fully. His rooms were luxurious, and his every whim catered to. Except one.

The woman last night, Isabelle Forster, intrigued him.

That she and her sister were not just the owners but also ran Forster Shipping captured his imagination.

He tugged on the bell pull and Fuchs—his manservant—entered the room. Langdon wasn't usually given to vacillations concerning clothes, but today he considered the choices his man laid out. The uniform he'd eschewed in favor of more casual and civilian options.

"You cannot go in there in your uniform, Major. The staff and citizens wouldn't stand for it. It's bad enough that you've been co-opted to their minds, to assist in the day-to-day operations," Arthur Davenport had complained in his gruff voice. "I had to pull a lot of strings to get you the position and out here without questions concerning your service."

Langdon had argued he was only there to investigate anomalies, but Davenport had remained adamant.

"You're there as a retired Major as far as anyone knows. You retain the rank of Major, but you're to wear civilian clothes, and no one must know the truth of your mission."

_ As he'd left Davenport's office, Langdon muttered, "It's not a bloody *social soiree." Not that it mattered, as the acting consul general had given him an order and he'd abide by that. After all, that's what you did in the army.*

Langdon waved to Fuchs, wordlessly agreeing to the gray pinstriped single-breasted coat and matching pants, the vest of figured Chinese silk, and the pale blue tie.

"Sir, your shirts are a little loose. The fashion is a slightly tighter fit." It was an ongoing discussion they had.

"Fashion be damned," Langdon groused, but Fuchs held his ground.

"Perhaps, sir, but civilian men notice these things. So do the ladies," Fuchs added in a dry tone.

Now Langdon started. "Surely not?"

His man nodded, and Langdon seethed.

"Fine. Do what you must then."

Fuchs smiled, a sly grin emerging. "You will require fitting, sir."

Langdon snarled as he stepped into his shoes. "Fine. Now, if you're done?"

"There are also several invitations, sir. If you'd peruse them and advise—"

He started then smiled, his man paling at the sight of his grin. "Leave them out, and I'll answer them all tonight."

If he didn't miss his guess the Fitzsimmons couple and Miss Forster would be welcomed into Shanghai society. He was also aware it was the interest he held in one Isabelle Forster that ultimately decided his entrée to society here in Shanghai, instead of merely rotating around it and dipping in a toe when it suited him.

"And Mrs. Elgin sent a message."

Langdon frowned. "Give it to me. I'll deal with it."

Mr. Elgin had passed three summers back, and in the last year, Langdon had been keeping company with the merry widow. Now, his interest in her was gone. Insignificant in the face of the beauty of Isabelle Forster.

It wasn't that he was vain, but Justina Elgin had honestly returned his sexual interest, and their relationship had endured through the winter, meeting both their needs. Now his had changed.

Instead of fiery green eyes, all he wanted was lively sapphire. Justina's full figure was surpassed by the willowy outline of Isabelle Forster.

He'd cut ties with Justina, though ensure her financial needs were met until she could find a way to be financially self-sufficient, but the situation between them must come to an end, he determined.

Accepting the coat from Fuchs, he left his rooms and headed for the office he inhabited, his mind engaged in considering the situation Davenport had insisted on him looking into.

Someone was importing opium to China through the Shanghai port using a commercial vessel. He knew the import came from India, yet many shipping lines plied those routes. Was it just one or many? There were still far more questions than answers, and even after months of covert investigations, there was little to go on.

The Chinese government had made it clear they desired an end to the trade. The British government had achieved the end they wanted and now wished to see the trade diminished, not that they made that information public.

After four months he'd not yet found any information on the where or how, and Davenport was becoming increasingly fractious about the situation.

Langdon hadn't long been at his desk when a missive appeared, summoning him to see the consul general. Davenport was a career diplomat; he knew precisely how to get the best out of his people and worked long hours to ensure he did. He also demanded immediate acquiescence, so Langdon packed up, hailed a cab, and made his way to the consulate building.

It was a rather traditional colonial building, constructed in the last ten years, and sought to impose itself on the skyline. Anyone who saw it knew it as a symbol of the empire, the white stark against the red stone entrances and gray of privately owned Chinese homes.

Langdon entered quickly, made himself known, and settled in to wait for Davenport's pleasure. It didn't take long, the man demanding he attend his office, and Langdon entered.

"Davenport, you summoned me."

The man opposite gestured that he sit, and Langdon did so, more to appease the frustrated man who groomed his whiskers absently while peering at the documents laying before him.

"Headway?" This was a man of few words, and Langdon sat back in the seat, feeling the back of the chair against his spine.

"Not yet, sir."

The man speared him with a glare, steepled his hands. "Aeddan Fitzsimmons, you've met him?"

"Yes."

"He's a spy, worked in India for the crown under Lytton. He's not a man to be trifled with, especially given his background."

Langdon waited for Davenport to expand on this, but he didn't. So Langdon directed the man to continue with a swift move of his hand.

"His wife and sister-in-law own and run Forster Shipping. There's been some chatter that Forster Shipping may be implicated in the opium mess. He'll protect his wife, and likely Miss Forster, so I don't think you can attack Fitzsimmons front-on. I do, however, hear the sister is comely. Perhaps she might be a way to find out more."

Langdon squirmed in his chair at the suggestion. "With all due respect, sir—"

Davenport speared him with a terse look. "Consider it an order, Deveraux. Romance the girl, find out what you can, and report back. The Chinese are making noises against us again, and until the new consul general is appointed, I'm trying to plug the gaps. The prime minister wants this dealt with. I want this dealt with." Now Davenport looked down and flicked through his sheaf of papers. "You're excused."

Langdon rose, wanting to remonstrate the concept of 'romancing' Isabelle Forster. If and when he did so, it would be under his own steam—not coerced by a government man. Then reality intruded.

He had orders.

Langdon turned and left the office.

In the three hours Isabelle had been here, she'd looked through the office, met the casual day staff, and taken stock of the systems they used to organize the warehouse, to prepare the shipments, and to process incoming cargo. It was mostly an acceptably run outpost of Forster Shipping.

Now, Isabelle stalked through the warehouse. "Show me the herbal medication, Staindhouse."

He scurried ahead of her as she inspected the large building. It was in reasonable repair, yet the floors were messy. Clods of mud and items that were yet to be packed into crates lay in piles. *Another thing to attend to.* Isabelle added it to her list of improvements for the man to undertake.

Staindhouse did his best, referring to the book he tucked under his arms. He waved her toward the rear corner, and they made their way in that direction.

Crates stacked three high faced her, roughly hewn but sturdy in her estimation. They should protect the contents over the long journey. The *Jamestown* would be taking them on later today, and she surveyed them, wondering what on earth they might contain.

One sat off to the side, and she pointed to it. "Open this one, Staindhouse."

He glanced around, searching for an implement. Then he took up a pry bar, and with a struggle and squeaking, popped the top.

She peered within. Jars nestled in their packing, and she lifted one, inspected it, then opened the top of the pot. "Mei, what is this?" The dried root reminded her of a carrot, though it was white.

The girl scurried over, glanced at the text, and sighed. "Ginseng, Miss."

"Ginseng? What is it used for?" Replacing the lid, she thrust it back, ensuring adequate padding surrounded it.

Mei smiled. "Many things. Shortness of breath and sleeping disorders are some." Isabelle turned to Staindhouse. "I see some improvements I'd like made. The warehouse appears well-constructed and cared for, however the interior," she said, waving her hand around, "does need work. If necessary, find a woman to clean it regularly. Next," and here she pointed to the piles of goods, "ensure everything is crated immediately. Items left on the floor become damaged, and that means less profit."

"Yes, Miss Forster." His head bobbed up and down.

"Before I leave, I'll prepare a list of things to attend to. Now, what I need you to do is find me a carriage—one in good repair. I will require one to travel from the house to the warehouse and for personal reasons, so ensure the driver is well compensated for being available when I require it."

His face screwed up with distaste. "There isn't much call for privately hired carriages, but I'll see what can be arranged."

Entering the office, she spied the time on the clock. "Oh dear, hail me a cab, as I must return to the house for lunch."

Isabelle would much rather have remained here and completed a full day of investigation. She'd already assessed the need to tidy the systems, and there was much to check with so few days remaining, but her sister would be waiting for her. Besides, any callers would expect her presence. An absence would surely be noted.

While she may well put in a full morning focusing on the business, the afternoons were not her own.

The man hurried out, and Isabelle donned the cloak and bonnet she'd removed on her arrival, then signaled Mei to follow just as a carriage moved to the door.

Staindhouse bowed low, and she thanked him for his attention then climbed into the conveyance. This one was cleaner and far newer than the one she'd traveled here in earlier. "Arrange a carriage for me tomorrow morning at eight. I will come directly."

Staindhouse nodded, then gave the driver directions to the house, and their transport jerked into movement.

She settled back against the squabs. "Tell me about your family, Mei."

The girl blanched. "I... Miss, I..."

Isabelle looked at the girl and took pity on her. "It's okay, Mei. I shouldn't have pushed." Once they arrived back at the house after an uncomfortably near-silent trip, Mei rushed to the door and opened it, just as Mrs. Hargraves reached the entry with a hand extended to latch. The look on the older woman's face was priceless, filled with surprise, but Isabelle kept quiet and smiled at her.

"You'll want to change, Miss," she said. "There are to be a few visitors after luncheon, I believe."

Jacinthe hovered at the top of the steps, her arms full of mending, and on a whim, Isabelle turned to Mrs. Hargraves. "Perhaps Mei could assist me?"

The woman frowned. "Well, I suppose so."

"Thank you," Isabelle answered and headed for the steps, Mei trailing behind.

The girl proved able if unskilled, and Isabelle, dressed in a dusky pink gown, eyed her reflection. Her cheeks had a glow that had been missing for months, her hair was tidy enough, and the necklet Mei had fastened around her throat completed the look.

Satisfied, she turned to Mei. "Have you assisted ladies before?"

Mei gave a small nod. "Sometimes. Usually, they bring their maids, and I help them." "You've done well," she praised the girl then rose. "Now, I should head down to lunch.

Go have your own, then come back and see if anything needs repairing. Jacinthe will attend to them."

*L*angdon was impatient. The hours passing slowly until he could present himself at the house on the edge of the concession. It wasn't personal interest, he assured himself, that only led him here. There was also a fair dollop of duty. Davenport had decreed his obedience. Therefore, he must attend to the matters as per the dictate of the consul general.

The hour of two in the afternoon had now come. He stepped up to the door and was received cordially, the housekeeper taking his cane and cloak. Then she ushered him to the room to the left again.

Mr. and Mrs. Fitzsimmons took tea with Miss Forster while Mrs. Markham and Mrs. Illey twittered. Once announced, Mrs. Fitzsimmons rose, but he waved her back down. "I do hope my calling is not inconvenient?"

"Not at all," answered Mrs. Fitzsimmons. "Mrs. Illey was just informing me that a musical evening is being arranged at

Lord Farnsworth's tomorrow, and Mrs. Markham invited us to a soiree on Friday."

"Of course, Major Deveraux, you are also invited."

Under normal circumstances, neither of those affairs were of interest, but if Miss Forster would be attending... He glanced in her direction, but she gave no indication.

"I'd be delighted," he answered, and the women twittered some more.

"Major, will you take tea?" Mrs. Fitzsimmons enquired, and he thanked her. A cup was sought, and tea poured.

Mrs. Markham and Mrs. Illey rose, making their goodbyes in short order, so only the four remained.

"So, Miss Isabelle, will you be attending?"

"Oh yes," she answered with a slight smile. "Society is so important." In her voice, he detected a note of sarcasm, and he had to restrain his smile.

"Then, perhaps you'd permit me to escort you?"

Now her eyes widened as Fitzsimmons cleared his throat.

Langdon knew he was pushing the boundaries of acceptable behavior, but if he didn't

move quickly, someone else would step in and his chance to complete the task assigned would disappear. He watched as she blushed just a little and nodded.

"I would appreciate that."

Fitzsimmons rose. "Perhaps you'd care to join me in the library, Deveraux." Langdon knew Fitzsimmons had no intention of sharing a cigar or a drink. Langdon

wished to remonstrate, but before the situation could move further, the door to the salon opened and in strode none other than Davenport himself.

"Well now, Mr. Fitzsimmons and Deveraux."

Mrs. Fitzsimmons rose again, but Davenport waved her back to her seat. He made introductions, and when Davenport turned to Isabelle, Langdon couldn't control the curling of his fingers into a fist.

"Will you introduce me?" Davenport enquired of Fitzsimmons, and the man did so.

Well aware of the etiquette of calling, Langdon waited then stood to make his farewells. Fitzsimmons walked him out. "What are you playing at, Deveraux?"

"Nothing. Miss Forster is delightful, and I wish to know her better." He took up his cane and coat from the housekeeper, but before he could reach the door, Fitzsimmons grabbed his arm.

"I have three sisters, Deveraux. I was there during their courting days, and your behavior is—"

Deveraux fought hard to contain himself. The frustration that built inside him, Davenport's orders, and now Fitzsimmons's comments fed the beast within his chest. He turned and eyeballed the man. "Miss Forster is a lady. I understand that. I find her interesting and would like to get to know her better. I am pressing my acquaintance, it's true, however, maybe you should allow her to decide what she wants." Every word dripped with disdain.

Langdon didn't wait for Fitzsimmons to answer. He merely bowed and retreated through the door before he said or did something unforgivable. At the bottom of the stairs, he stalked to the gate, ignored the carriage waiting beyond and walked, hoping to wash off some of the rage boiling inside himself. If Davenport hadn't made his demand, he would have taken more time with the woman. As it was, last night he'd seen her face in his dreams.

What would she be like if he took her in his arms? Soft and willing? Cold and haughty?

Instead of focusing on what he wanted now—Miss Isabelle Forster—he had to cast off a lover who no longer interested him, find out who the hell was importing opium, and attend a society function.

Joy.

Chapter Four

ISABELLE VACILLATED. "Mei, do I wear the sapphire blue with the lace edging or the green with gold embroidery? What say you?"

The girl looked at her and frowned. "Some Chinese would say blue is the color of illness, while green is the color of vitality. On you though, the blue reminds me of waters that run deep, of secrets. The green makes your skin pale. I would choose blue."

Catching the fitted blue gown against herself, Isabelle whirled to face the mirror. "It does suit me well. Perhaps I should give the green away? I didn't like it when it was being suggested, but I allowed Lady Manton to talk me into it." She eyed the gown then turned to Mei. "Will it fit you?"

The girl backed away. "I don't wear English clothes. Otherwise, I'll be in trouble. My father forbids it."

Isabelle felt the narrowing of her eyes. *I shall have to find out who her father is and why he allows her to work but only dressed in Chinese clothing. After all, she also has English heritage.*

"Would you help me into the gown?" she requested of the girl, aware that Major Deveraux would be there soon.

The girl scurried about, fastening her into the gown then

attending to her hair. Isabelle had decided to wear it up, in a simple snood. Mei fastened the circlet of silver around Isabelle's neck, which was the only adornment. Then Isabelle slid her feet into the slippers which matched her gown.

On the bed lay gloves, bag, fan, and wrap, and she gathered them up. "Pack the green gown and its accessories away. I'll deal with them later," she told the girl with a smile. "Then down to dinner with you."

Once through the door, Isabelle took a deep, calming breath, smoothed down her gown, and descended the staircase. Below Major Deveraux already waited as did Elspeth and Aeddan.

His eyes turned to hers, and even at this distance, between them lay more than just a glint of interest.

As much as she wanted to ignore that glow on his visage, there was an answering one within her breast. He looked dashing with his dark hair under the glittering lights of the chandelier. His formal clothing, black with only a hint of gold and silver at the buttons, fitted him perfectly, and the flash of white from his shirt shone under the lights. The cut and color choices accentuated his dramatic good looks. It was hard to hold her hand steady on the stairs while emotions boiled within her, but somehow, she managed it.

He reached out for her as she stepped onto the tiles of the foyer. His hand curled around hers, and heat suffused her.

"Miss Forster." He bowed, his eyes firmly fastened on hers.

"Major Deveraux." Even to herself, her voice sounded breathless.

Elspeth and Aeddan watched. She could feel the intensity of their stares on her, but it didn't break the spell that wove between herself and the major.

He straightened, granted her a smile that made her insides quiver, and tucked her hand into his arm, and they turned, Aeddan and Elspeth leading the way. They climbed into the carriage, and the major handed her in also. It rocked and swayed, heading down the drive and through the gates.

The silence stretched between them. It wasn't fraught like someone trying to come up with something to say. Instead, it wove around her, enveloping her in the sensual web that had been growing ever more intricate since they met.

It was a short drive, but when they reached the residence, there was a wait.

"You look beautiful tonight, Miss Forster." The timbre of his voice was dark and subtly dangerous.

"Thank you. And you look quite dashing."

The carriage rolled forward, and the door opened. The footman handing her out, and he followed. Up the steps and into the grand house they processed. Aeddan and Elspeth hovered ahead of them, then finally the footman turned to them. Langdon gave his name, and they entered the house.

The music was as bad as he'd expected. The woman singing in falsetto was more vibrato than comfortable, the key slightly off and her bosom fit to explode from her gown. Langdon watched as Miss Forster attempted a creditable interest, though it too had waned by the third song. When the set of pieces were complete, there was polite clapping, and an audible sigh of thankfulness rippled through the assemblage.

A gentleman settled at the piano, and clearly, he was far more accomplished. Those assembled in the room rose to partake of the refreshments, and Langdon held out his arm to Isabelle. "A drink, Miss Forster?"

"Yes, please."

He ushered her to the table, lifting a glass of champagne for each of them.

"Thank you, Major."

They moved beside the window, and he looked out onto the garden. In the distance, he could make out the outline of ships on the horizon, the rigging moving in the chilly January breeze.

"You appear to enjoy running Forster Shipping," he commented.

She turned and smiled. "I do indeed. While it is unusual for a younger woman to be in a position of authority in this world, I welcome the challenge. My father trained both my older sister and I. Our youngest sister had shown no real interest or, dare I say, aptitude for such matters. I find manifests and crew organization, routes, and timetables interesting. I enjoy perusing and checking the ledgers. This last year or so, I've had opportunities to do things that I couldn't have done in England."

"You're comfortable in your role."

"Yes," Isabelle agreed. "Though the restrictions of society chafe."

He admired a woman who spoke her mind. That Miss Isabelle could do that yet fit into society and was a beauty didn't challenge his manhood. That was unlike many others who professed modernity.

Too many men restricted their wives and daughters. They were expected to settle into a pattern of genteel servility. He considered himself far more advanced than that. Forward-thinking even.

Even as he considered the concept, others crowded around. They demanded introductions, which he carefully gave, all the while keeping Isabelle's arm on his. The men noted his proprietary actions, and the women giggled vacuously. His nerves tightened like the bow on a violin. Instead of showing the frustration, he smiled and cajoled those surrounding them, ensuring no one knew what was going on inside. Keeping up the façade was necessary though trying.

Isabelle, meanwhile, took it all in her stride, as if born to the aristocracy. He twisted his lips, aware that he, an aristocrat by birth but a soldier by choice, was far less comfortable in these surroundings.

"Perhaps we might make an occasion of it," Miss Pembroke prodded, and he realized he'd lost the thread of the conversation.

"I'm only here for a limited time. Otherwise, I'm sure I would have enjoyed the adventure," Miss Forster replied.

He wondered at her words. *Limited time.* He'd best find out what that meant exactly. But not now, as they were being called in to supper.

Chapter Five

THE PACE at which Isabelle worked could hardly be called break-neck. On Wednesday, after the musicale, Elspeth and Isabelle returned the calls to the women and men who'd left cards. Thursday evening they spent with Mr. Grayson, Mr. Davenport, and Lord Huntingdon. Friday evening was the soiree at Mrs. Markham's. On Saturday Isabelle spent the entire day with Elspeth, visiting the local stores, met with a dressmaker and endured fittings, ensuring her sister could expand her wardrobe to allow for the increasing size of her waistline. Sunday was a day of rest, so she brooded at home, more than slightly aware that Staindhouse would be occupied and she was loathe to intrude on his time with his wife.

The ledgers now up-to-date, she was working her way through the list of suppliers, making notes as to what needed to increase and where they might better utilize their cargo space.

"You should take a break, my dear," Aeddan said just over her shoulder.

"I have much to do and so little time. Each afternoon we are either receiving or visiting, and almost every night is socially restricted."

Aeddan sighed and settled in the seat in the parlor she'd come to think of as her study. "You don't wish to leave so soon, do you?"

Laying down the pen, Isabelle studied her brother-in-law. She knew him as a caring and considerate husband. A man of loyalty and strength, and a brother whom she now adored. But he didn't understand that she wanted and needed more, because it wasn't the way he was made.

"Aeddan, I feel that when I return to England, I'll once more become the meek and mild Miss Forster. The spinster aunt who visits and brings gifts to lavish upon nieces and nephews. The sister who is quietly stoic while everyone around her lives a life." The words tumbled forth, betraying her frustration at her sex.

A knock at the door had them both turning, and Elspeth entered the room, looking wan. The illness each morning was taking its toll on her at this point.

"There you both are."

Aeddan grimaced. "Isabelle was telling me what she fears will become of her life when we return to England. I didn't understand—"

Isabelle reached out and grasped his arm. "It's hard for a man to know how we live as spinsters. While Elspeth was there, I was, if not content, then at least resigned to my fate as I would have someone to share that future with."

Elspeth dropped into an empty seat. "You don't wish to accompany us?"

"But you won't be alone," added Aeddan.

Now it was Isabelle's turn to sigh. "It's not that I don't want to, I just want to see what more there is. I want to fulfill myself and explore this land, as you did in India, Elspeth." She bit back the last sentence. *I want to find a love as you have.* It wasn't Elspeth's fault she had not yet found what completed her.

Liar! Her brain screamed the correction. She had met

someone. Isabelle was sure she could find all her sister had and more, but the restrictions placed on her stopped the kind of relationship she yearned for from growing. Instead, it was the time constraints of Aeddan's father and Elspeth's health that took point. Her own now secondary to everyone else's needs.

The zing of pleasure she felt every time Langdon touched her would remain nothing more than a memory. The cold ball in her belly grew a little larger at that thought.

Isabelle thought back to the book she'd seen in Elspeth's room on their return from the adventure in India. The one wrapped in purple silk. It was filled with explicit yet oddly compelling images.

She couldn't honestly say if that was quite what she wanted, but the passion that leaped off the illustration on each page called to a hunger inside her.

Elspeth rose, and her actions jerked Isabelle from her introspection. The pain on her face was clawing at Isabelle. "I'm so sorry, dearest. If only—"

Unable to contain her sigh, Isabelle held up her hand to stop her sister's protestations. "No, Elspeth. I'm the one who should be apologizing. I didn't mean to bring all of this to you."

Isabelle looked at the book on the table, then closed it, well aware that there were no options or choices. Discussing it only made the situation worse, because it made her think about the opportunities lost.

"I should go upstairs and change." She rose and headed for the door, laying her hand on the knob, for a moment hoping to escape the inevitable. She had to go home with Aeddan and Elspeth, because a single woman couldn't stay by herself. Regrets just made things worse.

On her way up the hall, she spied Mrs. Hargraves and stopped. "A moment if I may, Mrs. Hargraves?"

The woman turned with a smile and welcomed her into

the dining room as she continued straightening the table. "Yes, Miss Isabelle?"

"Mei. Tell me about her."

Mrs. Hargraves's face fell. "She's a good girl. I'd vouch for her."

Isabelle shook her head at the defense in the woman's tone. "No, she's excellent. I'm just wondering about some of the things she's told me. She's half-Chinese?"

The housekeeper nodded and bit her lip. "Yes."

"Who is her father?"

Mrs. Hargraves glanced over her shoulder, eyes wide, as if checking to ensure no one was listening. "He's an Englishman is all I know for sure, Miss Isabelle. But she's been in service here for three years, and as I said, I'd vouch for her."

Isabelle wondered at the lack of information. Mei hadn't been precisely forthcoming, and she did wonder if Mrs. Hargraves knew more than she was saying.

Mrs. Hargraves sighed. "I believe he's running transport up and down the Yang-tzu Chiang, even though it's not allowed, and he brings in girls. Some say that he buys them. Sells them to unscrupulous men."

Isabelle couldn't contain her shock. "Buys them?"

The woman nodded. "Mei's mother was one of the first he brought downriver not long after he arrived. Some say he's a cast-off son who never mended his ways, and others say he's a ruffian from the stews of London. Anyway, he kept Mei's mother long enough to have the child. Then he kept the girl. When she was about fourteen, he turned her out and told her she wasn't much use to him. She came here looking for work, and he demands that whatever she makes, she must hand over to him."

"I see," Isabelle said. "He still rules her life."

"Yes, well, once she was employed, he decided she was useful. He takes all her money. Treats her poorly, and sometimes he hits her—I've seen the bruising myself. She's deathly afraid of him."

"I see. I wonder, if I wished to employ her as my lady's maid, she'd need to reside here all the time. Do you think she'd be interested?"

Mrs. Hargraves stared at Isabelle. "Miss?"

"Well, my sister has her maid, and there are times it's difficult to rely on her. Mei already has many skills, and she's growing used to the way I like things done."

"Mayhap you should ask her yourself."

Isabelle nodded. "Yes. I think I shall."

On that, she turned and headed through the door, but not quickly enough that she didn't hear Mrs. Hargraves mumbling, "You could do worse than Mei."

As Isabelle made her way up the stairs, she thought long and hard. She didn't just want Mei while they were in Shanghai. In her mind, it made sense that Mei should come home with her too.

Except that was a big request, and she wasn't sure it was one Mei was ready for just yet. So Isabelle decided to wait for the right time to broach the subject with the young woman.

"Small steps first, Isabelle," she muttered and opened the door to her chamber.

Monday came, and Langdon woke, his mind whirring with ideas. Tonight was the ball at the consulate. As had now become his normality, he'd be escorting Miss Forster to the event. He hoped that she'd allow him some time alone in the gardens.

His man, Fuchs, fretted about his shirt while he concentrated on other, more vital tasks.

He made an appointment to meet with one of his informants to receive information on the opium smuggling ring and also arranged to meet with his banker at the Oriental Bank, who handled transactions for him of a personal nature.

By eleven in the morning, he was safely ensconced inside the building, waiting to meet with the banker. He took a seat and twirled his hat, his ornate cane propped beside him on the heavy wooden pew.

Not for the first time, he wished his uniform was a suitable mode of dress for his position. Then he wouldn't have to deal with much of the folderol associated with the current fashionable attire. Fuchs would no doubt fret about creases, but he'd been assured his uniform may create more questions than he was currently able to answer, so he'd complied.

The tap of feet on the floor caught his attention, and Langdon rose.

"Major? It's a pleasure to meet you. We received your request this morning and have cleared the time to deal with your account," the man babbled, mopped his face, then breathed deeply. "Please come through, Major," the banker invited, and Langdon followed the man into a small office.

The short, gray-haired man with an enormous mustache and ill-fitting suit appeared quite uncomfortable, his face taking on a florid red. Langdon knew he'd been apprised of his title, his man of business having impressed that on the owners when he'd arranged for monies to be transferred to the holdings here in Shanghai.

It also meant Langdon couldn't tell if the discomfort was due to his title and refusal to use it, or it was more to do with the sums of money Langdon had at his disposal.

A young woman entered. "Tea, Mr. Bilson?"

The man stared at Langdon, silently waiting for an answer.

"Ah, no. This will only be a short visit," Langdon replied.

Once the door closed with a click, Bilson looked at Langdon, a trickle of sweat sliding over his bulbous cheeks, having been missed by the mopping exercise, quill in hand. "Well,

Major, this is quite a surprise, to be sure. How may we assist you today?"

"I have concluded a very satisfactory arrangement with one Mrs. Elgin. In light of the, shall we say, relationship between us, I wish to make provision for her. I believe the sum of three hundred pounds should be sufficient."

The man gaped at him, blinking once, twice, then a third time. "Three hundred pounds? That seems somewhat excessive, sir." The man glanced away, then shuffled papers on the desk, as if avoiding looking directly at Langdon.

Langdon reclined back in his seat, aware the man was out of his depths in his attempts to correct the sum which Langdon was more than happy to settle. "Under normal circumstances. However, I wish to ensure a clean break. I am not settling a house, servants, or even lavish amounts of jewels."

The man harrumphed and made a note.

Langdon steepled his hands on his chest. "I realize this is not the generally accepted way of such things. However, I have reasons which may or may not become apparent, Bilson."

Bilson stood. "I won't be long then, sir." He scurried out of sight and returned sometime later. "I have arranged for an account be created, sir, as you've indicated. If you'd sign for this document?"

Langdon took the outstretched writing implement without a word and inspected the parchment noting the transfer of three hundred pounds to an account for one Mrs. Justina Elgin. The quill felt smooth from use as Langdon scribbled his name on the receipt. "You really should upgrade to fountain pens. I hear they are much easier to use than conventional quills."

Now the man stared at him, mouth agape. "Fountain pen?"

"Ah, well, I'm sure in time." Langdon reached out and

took the receipt's copy from Bilson's hand. "I will ensure she presents herself shortly to finalize any formalities."

He lifted his hat, slipped it onto his head, and rose from the chair, feeling better about his actions before striding from the bank.

In the street, he glanced left and right. He hailed a cab and gave the direction of Mrs. Elgin's. He could do this in a cowardly fashion and send her a note and the receipt, but he'd determined she deserved at least the courtesy of being informed to her face that their brief alliance had concluded.

He alighted, gave the driver the request to wait, and walked up to the door of her house. It wasn't massive or ornate. Some might even describe it as a slightly shabby, two-story boarding house. She wasn't a woman of means, but she was a lady by birth, the daughter and widow of a gentleman.

The door opened at his knock, and her maid ushered him into the hall, offering to take his hat and cane, but he disagreed. "Mrs. Elgin? Is she home?"

"Yes, Major, if you'd follow me."

They walked the few steps to the small room she used for entertaining at the front of the house, and he entered. Justina Elgin sat in one of the two winged chairs by the fire, her fingers plying a needle.

"Why, Langdon, this is a surprise." She rose, but he waved her back into her seat. Discomfort spread through him. "Justina, I apologize for interrupting—"

"Not at all, Langdon. Won't you sit?"

He shook his head. "No. I won't stay. I..."

Her eyes grew wide. "We're done then, are we?" She rose anyway, putting aside her mending and taking a step toward him. "I always knew at sometime this would be the case. Thank you for coming to see me. For telling me face-to-face rather than sending a note."

He fidgeted, suddenly uncomfortable with what came

next. "Justina, you have acted at all times with grace. I wanted to thank you and, in some way, offer you some security."

"Pshaw," she remonstrated, but he shook his head.

"No. I wish to help you. I know your situation is uncertain. As a friend, I wish to assist you. I have, therefore, made arrangements with the Oriental Bank. An account has been created to assist you financially."

Red flags adorned her cheeks. "Langdon, why would you do that?" Embarrassment colored her voice.

"Because your children's education is draining your finances. I know your precarious situation has forced you to lease this property after selling your home, yet you cannot return home to England because your late husband's debts were extreme."

She covered her mouth with a hand.

"I want to help you, my dear. There are three hundred pounds available to you. Enough to go home, to purchase a small house and pay for your daughters' education. As a friend, without any restrictions or ties."

"You're buying me off?" Her voice choked at the end of the query.

"No!" He strode forward, wondering if there was a more natural way to explain that he felt, in some small way, that he could make amends for ending their affair so abruptly. "If you'd prefer it to be a gift or loan, then so be it. I just want you to be happy. I know you've said many times you wished you could afford to travel back home but you can't. You told me your husband's estate had collapsed and left you with debts that you were only able to pay off once you disposed of the house. Let me help you now."

Tears shone in her eyes. "Why?"

On a sigh, he reached out a hand and laid it on her shoulder. He was willing her to understand. "Because that's what friends do. And I consider you a friend." He pulled back, hunted through his pocket for the paper. When he had it in his hand, he gave her the receipt. "Go to the bank. Make yourself known to Bilson there and show him this. That's all I ask."

Her lips trembled. "I would never have asked this from you."

"That's why I would choose no other way of thanking you. You didn't ask or grasp. There were no requests for jewelry or gewgaws during our time together. You're a lady, and I would see you treated as such."

Her sob split the air, discomforting him.

He bowed deeply, then raised up and looked her in the eye. "Goodbye, Justina." Langdon turned and slowly retreated to the door, then stopped, turned with one last searching look. "I wish you all the best, my friend." Then he left.

Frustration ate at Isabelle. The *Jackson* had set sail and three of the crates had been left on the dock. "How on earth were they overlooked?" she demanded of Staindhouse.

He reddened further. "I can't say, Miss Forster. I gave directions to the men to load them and met with the bankers as you requested. When I returned, they were there and the *Jackson* already at sail in the harbor."

"Have them brought in, then I wish to meet with the stevedores."

She marched into the building, well aware that she'd already created a scene worthy of retelling. Nothing about this situation made sense. The books appeared in order, Staindhouse seemed to be competent, and he'd been addressing an issue she'd raised when the incident took place.

So why were these crates overlooked?

Vexed, she directed Mei to prepare tea as she settled herself at the desk, head aching as she realized there was nothing more to be done until the next ship was due, in several weeks.

The door chimed, and Isabelle looked up as two burly men entered the office. "You wished to see us, Miss Forster?"

They removed their hats and waited as she rose. "Yes. I wish to know how three crates could be overlooked during the final loading of the *Jackson*."

The first man shifted uncomfortably, while the second nudged him. "See, loading day is chaotic, Miss. Once all the crates are lined up, we arrange them to be loaded into the cargo bay. Somehow, we had more, like those on the side weren't marked with the red cross Mr. Staindhouse usually puts on them. So, when we was finished, we checked. No mark, no load."

Isabelle frowned. "Are they usually marked before they are sent to the dock?"

"Yes, Miss Forster. Mr. Staindhouse, he's most specific like. He hisself marks them with this paint. These weren't marked, so we didn't have to load them, Mr. Staindhouse told us when we started." He hopped from foot to foot, clearly concerned that she'd punish or even sack him.

"Is this the first time this has happened?"

"Miss?" questioned the second man.

"Yes?"

"Begging your pardon, Miss Forster, but we ain't comfortable discussing—"

Ire raised, Isabelle silently counted backward from ten. "I am an owner of Forster Shipping. I oversee all cargos and staffing and have done so for several years. When I ask a question, I expect an honest and immediate answer. Is this the first time this has occurred?" Ice infused her words, and the man blanched.

The older man, who'd answered all the other questions, shook his head. "Yes, Miss. This is the first time."

He looked sincere, and Isabelle made a mental note to

discuss it with Staindhouse. She nodded. "I see." She pondered his words a little further. The timing was indeed strange. Why now? Was it a coincidence or something more? "For now, go. I'll continue my investigation on what happened today."

They left, the younger man muttering about women and not knowing their place while the older man hissed to him to be silent. Isabelle ignored the outburst, her mind occupied with checking the contents of the crates in the ledger to ascertain if they'd survive the extra storage time.

All shipping companies experienced losses. On a purely business level, that was a cost that needed to be absorbed into prices agreed upon when selling the items. But when it was the result of carelessness or poor practices, then it left her wondering if there was a hiccup in the system. If so, how easily could that be overcome?

She settled down to examine the loading book, seeking the numbers which were burned into the wood of the crates, her fingertips sliding down columns. "Three hundred forty-one, three hundred forty-two..." The numbers weren't listed. "Odd."

Mei entered the room, carrying the teapot and cups she'd requested. Isabelle firmed her lips, the whole time her gaze on the docks beyond the door. *Three crates. None of the numbered crates were listed in the cargo manifest. They'd been left on the docks after the loading was complete. Why? What did they contain, and why were they there? Where had they come from, because they weren't in the warehouse previously according to any records she could locate.*

Isabelle decided she'd answer one of the questions after tea. She'd ask Staindhouse to open them for inspection. Then she'd make arrangements for them to be stored or dealt with. But the other answers remained unknown. Unknowns made her anxious, and anxiety infuriated her.

"I'll find those answers," she promised herself as she took a sip of tea.

Chapter Six

LANGDON TWITCHED his tie one last time. "Fuchs?" He sought his valet's approbation in the matter of his dress.

The man nodded. "You'll do, sir." Fuchs stood back, his eyes wandering over Langdon, checking for any imperfection, but the satisfied smirk told Langdon what he needed to know.

Nervousness was an emotion Langdon felt unfamiliar with. The fact that tonight—a ball of all things—made his stomach quiver and his mind ready to splinter in a million different locations spoke volumes about his level of unease.

No woman ever affected him as much as Miss Isabelle Forster.

It wasn't her beauty, though any man could become breathless with her delicate features, sapphire blue eyes, and rosebud lips. It wasn't her spirit, though that too was clearly discernable, as she traveled about with a young maid only in a foreign country without fear to docks of all places. It had to be something intrinsic in her. An amalgam of her honesty of character, her forthright nature, and her commitment to the shipping company mixed into the other positive traits she exhibited.

She'd been attending the wharf-side office six days a week.

His man on the scene assured him she'd taken a keen interest in the cargo and ordering, the building, and even the staff. It was unusual in a woman, yet it didn't detract from her finer qualities. He knew she danced with grace, having now squired her several times in a variety of social settings. She could maintain a sensible conversation without being labeled a bluestocking. Her skills were equal to any of his sisters and members of the nobility. No, everything about her was—he hunted for the correct term—impeccable.

He sighed heavily, took up his cane, and turned to Fuchs. "Don't wait up. I'll attend to myself."

He left the room, taking the stairs to the ground floor two at a time. The sound of leather echoing of marble treads filling the curious silence. They may be in China, but the house was a modern marvel of European innovation.

The carriage he'd commandeered for the night was waiting at the curb, and he climbed in. The sound of hooves and the wheels rolling along the ground settled him a little. He allowed himself to concentrate on the sounds, let them soothe his ragged thoughts. At the house, the carriage turned up the drive, wheeling smoothly into place.

The door opened, and he alighted, sucked in a lungful of air, and made his way up the steps.

The access to the house opened smoothly, a footman alerted to his presence standing by, and he stepped within.

In the vaulted foyer, Fitzsimmons offered him a hand to shake and indicated he should enter the parlor. Mrs. Fitzsimmons perched on the edge of the chaise, her gown of green silk adorned with lace and silk flowers in pink and red. Her radiance was a pleasure to behold as she took his hand in welcome.

He accepted a drink from Mr. Fitzsimmons, turning at a sound, and the door opened. When he glanced to see what the noise heralded, Isabelle entered.

His mind splintered as he beheld what to him appeared to

be a goddess. Her gown a vision of beauty. The two tones of blue flowing like a waterfall to the floor from the fitted bodice. It alternated from blush to the same radiant sapphire as her eyes. The bodice molded over her figure, the bustle decorated with the same silver foil as the rosettes adorning the tiny caplets on her upper arms. The gown draped artfully over her bosom, which rose and fell, capturing his attention before his gaze settled on her face.

Her golden hair was coiffed so that the locks formed ringlets entwined with ribbon and rosettes to match the accessories of her gown. Around her neck lay a single necklet of diamonds and sapphires alternated with the fleur-de-lis of enameled silver.

His heart lurched.

Mrs. Fitzsimmons rose. "You look absolutely beautiful, my darling."

Mr. Fitzsimmons beamed. "Indeed, you look exceedingly well, Isabelle."

His brain whirred back into life. "Radiant." Langdon bowed deeply then extended his hand. "Ravishing." She placed her hand in his, and he kissed the back of it, aware of the frisson of connection between them.

The smile she gifted him filled him with warmth as she settled into the chaise beside her sister. She accepted a glass of sparkling liquid and sipped. He and Fitzsimmons seated themselves in the high wing chairs with tonic waters. The conversation rolled around him, and he only answered as prompted, his thoughts turning inward as he considered the woman he'd be escorting. She'd stolen his thoughts when she'd entered the room, and his primitive instincts flared to life. She was his and would remain that way.

Once they'd finished their drinks, they rose, the women donning their wraps and taking up their evening bags, and they proceeded from the house, climbing into the carriage he'd arranged.

*W*as it simply a moment in time, Isabelle wondered as she settled into the carriage beside him. Or was there a deeper connection between them?

Langdon Deveraux exuded a masculinity that left her heart fluttering and more besides.

She'd seen the interest Elspeth had been unable to ignore with Aeddan when they'd first met and even immediately after their marriage. Isabelle was sure that the emotions that warred inside her were more intense than anything Elspeth had experienced with Aeddan. Surely no one else could feel what she did right now?

As much as she'd attempted to stem those stirrings, his constant presence, his thoughtfulness all fed the needs she felt. Every night he'd squired her to a social event that Elspeth deemed acceptable. He'd ensured the carriage was ready for her use when she required it.

At events, he'd danced attendance, kept her plied with morsels and drinks, and ensured she met those socially acceptable while shielding her from those who were beyond the pale. Each morning a missive arrived, a token thanking her for the evening before, and more than once, it came with a floral tribute.

The first time she'd been baffled and surprised. It was as if he knew her daily plans, ensuring the items arrived well before she could leave. Now, she looked forward to the notelets and kept them within her jewelry casket. More than once—like a schoolgirl—she'd fished them out and re-read every word. The print bold etched into the paper was sturdy and reminiscent of the man who sent them. Assured. Confident.

Nighttimes were the absolute worst, as the dreams of him became more intense. The first had surprised her, though each night the yearnings grew harder to ignore. Even now, the first dream played through her head.

"Major?" she whispered into the wind.

He parted the foliage of the gardens, the fragrance of many flowers filling the air, and when he smiled at her, the knot in her belly tightened. "Isabelle, come with me."

She'd taken his hand, hers shaking in his grip as he tugged her closer.

Their lips touched in a soft caress, and she melted into his arms...

Last night, there'd been a much greater intensity to the dream kiss, and not for the first time she had the sensation of heat and need curling in her belly. An ache forming in a place she never expected to experience. Asking Elspeth for advice was out of the question, so instead, she'd plagued herself with vague recollections from the chatter of maids years ago.

For all she'd listened, there was no talk of emotional attachment to the males involved. Those long-ago conversations had been heavy with 'petting' and 'oh, it felt so wicked.' No help at all.

That wasn't the only thing causing Isabelle angst. When she thought about the possibility of returning to England with Elspeth and Aeddan, pain radiated from her chest—shattering in its intensity. She wasn't ready to leave behind any opportunity with Langdon Deveraux.

On arrival at the consulate, she waited to be handed out, her arm taken by the man who made her shiver.

"Cold?" he inquired.

"No. Just nerves," Isabelle prevaricated.

They were announced and entered the room. The crowd was loud and craning as if hoping to catch sight of the woman on the major's arm. Isabelle wondered if she'd missed a part of womanly understanding.

More than one female smiled, though the gesture appeared pained or a little strained. "Major, do you attend many of these social functions?" Isabelle asked.

He steered her down the steps into the ballroom. "No. Not really."

She blinked, bamboozled by his answer.

When the major introduced her to a knot of people gathered at the bottom of the stairs, she smiled, curtseyed, and made small talk.

"So, my dear, I hear you're in trade," tittered one of the younger women, her eyes artfully wide—though to Isabelle's mind, the action was affected. "I declare, it would be beyond me to even know where to begin! I mean, before anything else, dealing with those men! It must be a most painful experience."

She'd heard variations of the wording before, and with some years of experience, she brushed it off. "Oh, it just takes practice." Isabelle kept her smile polite and waited to move on, which happened with a sharp look from the major to the woman.

"I apologize. Miss Thorne can be somewhat—"

Her fingers clenched on his arm. "No, Major. There is no need for that. I have faced this before, and it says more about them than about the person they direct their lack of understanding toward."

Only a portion of the stiffness wore away; the way his body had hardened beneath her touch during the nasty comments surprised her, as did the need to soothe him. It was both troubling and difficult to dispel.

They continued their slow promenade of the room. Isabelle didn't accept any offers for her dance card, and while Langdon had enquired after the first hint of interest from others, she waved him away. "I'm a little fatigued this evening."

"You are well?" The major's inquiry had her touching his hand.

"Yes. I just find the evening events tiring."

The gentlemen accepted her response with a smile and a slight bow.

On reaching the window, she bit her lip, waved the fan which hung from a ribbon at her wrist, and protested the heat inside the room. The major obliged her in opening the door, and they stepped out on the balcony.

She turned with a sigh. "Major."

He reached for her, his gloved hand warm. She took it, and he drew her down the stairs into the shadows. Steadied her as she nearly tripped on the last stair. "Miss Forster, allow me." The sound of his voice changed and deepened.

Inside her body, a seed of hope took root as he slid his hands gently up her arms and tugged her close.

"Tell me you don't want this, and I'll step away," he said.

Want. Such a dangerous word. "I do." Two small words, but like a tether, dragging her toward him. She felt herself sway, his hands heavy on her shoulders.

The glint in his eyes—dark and sensually risky—warned her that she'd be playing with fire, yet there was no turning back now. She embraced the danger as he leaned in.

"I've wanted to do this since I met you, Miss Forster." The whisper of his breath on her lips was a shock which encouraged her.

"Then don't stop, Major," she whispered.

His arms encircled her, tugging her so that her front snuggled up against him.

The feel of his lips, full and warm against her own, was a shock. When they opened and closed over hers, a myriad of sensations flickered through her. A wild pleasure thrummed in her chest, while a curl of heat and heaviness strangely pooled in her abdomen.

The major tugged back a little, and his hand framed her cheek, a soft thumb caressing in mesmerizing circles. "Kiss me back," he instructed.

Isabelle blinked. "I... I don't know how."

A grin grew on his face, wolfishly arrogant. "Then I'll teach you, Isabelle. I can call you Isabelle, can't I?"

It was as if she'd been hypnotized, but Isabelle nodded.

"Yes," she breathed, not wanting to break the spell between them.

"And you shall call me Langdon," he murmured as his gaze dropped to her lips.

"Langdon," Isabelle parroted.

"Now, when I put my lips on yours, let them open. Close your eyes and listen to your body."

Her eyes slid shut as his lips once more claimed hers. This time she let her mouth open, felt the shock of his tongue surging deep, and she moaned, because there was no other way to show her pleasure at the intimate gesture.

The demands of Isabelle's body took over, demanding that she become a partner in this wicked dance. Her tongue slid against his, while the wild thunder of her veins demanded more. She yearned for him to touch her in ways she didn't yet understand.

Langdon pulled away, and she sucked in an unsteady breath.

"No more," he said, his voice deep and masculine, the movement of his whispered words sliding over her sensitive flesh. She shivered, and he pulled her against him. "We should go inside," he murmured.

"Not... Not yet, Major." Isabelle could feel the flaming of her face and cupped her cheeks with her hands.

"Langdon," he corrected her.

"Oh, well in private, perhaps, Langdon." The intimacy of the situation a welcome revelation as pleasure suffused her. "I require a moment."

He laughed as she checked her hair and turned away, seeking a moment to compose herself.

"You're perfect, Isabelle." There was no laughter this time. Only the voice that made her tingle all the way through. She whisked around and noted the intensity of his gaze. "Perfect."

He took her hand and led her back up the steps, as she considered what he said. At the top, she stilled. "Langdon?"

He shook his head. "Not now. We'll talk tomorrow." Then he turned and led her back to the ball.

*I*gnoring the ache of his body, Langdon focused on the social chit-chat, the etiquette of squiring the most beautiful woman in the room, and ensuring no buck invaded what he now considered as his territory.

The luscious woman, Isabelle Forster, had entered Shanghai society, taking it by storm. Every man wanted to talk to her. Every woman either wanted to be seen by her side or alternately wished to scorn her for the trade she remained involved in. He categorized those who'd scorn her as weak-minded and unworthy of any further interest.

Since the scorching kiss, the primitive part of his brain had demanded he take her back to his rooms, to brand her and keep her. Of course, that wasn't in the least bit acceptable in today's highly advanced society. So he fought the sexual urges with all his might.

By the end of the evening, he'd stretched his urbanity to the hilt and required time to recover. There was the carriage ride home, close enough that she'd be able to snuggle up against him.

Fitzsimmons watched him the entire trip back to the house, then invited him inside on the pretext of a nightcap.

He had no illusions what that would be. They entered Fitzsimmons's library, the man filling two glasses with a deep colored brandy.

"Isabelle. Your interest in her has been noted. Tonight, you both disappeared from the ballroom." Fitzsimmons lowered himself into a seat, indicated Langdon should do the same, and took a sip of the liquor.

Langdon waited, hoping by drawing the silence out that

the man would change the subject, but alas, that was not the case. Fitzsimmons was a master of silence.

Now he sighed. "I'm unsure. I am intrigued by her."

Fitzsimmons continued waiting in silence.

Langdon slumped. "What would you have me do?"

The man took another drink of his brandy. "Isabelle is a strong woman, much like her sister. But she's the last of the sisters unmarried. She struggles with loneliness. I am not unaware that it will be worse when she returns to England. Louisa is married with a child on the way, and Elspeth and I..." He broke off, and Langdon nodded.

He too had sisters who'd been unmarried until later in life, and he knew the frustrations they had endured. The quiet confinement they railed against.

"I would wish to know her better before I..."

Fitzsimmons reclined in his seat, sliding his glass onto the tabletop. "There is but two weeks before we leave, Deveraux. Many men choose a life partner with less. For the likes of you and I, these decisions will change the course of our lives."

Considering Fitzsimmons's words was a jolt. "I don't yet know." "There's still time, friend. But it's running out."

Langdon finished his drink and took his leave.

Chapter Seven

RISING LATE THE NEXT MORNING, Isabelle lazed abed, considering last night's kiss. It had been so much more than she'd expected. The dream-kiss ethereal beside reality. He'd been tender at first, then increased the sensation until she'd been awash with a pang of hunger which roared through her veins.

Even now, when she touched her fingers to her lips, the taste of him lingered. Exotic and spicy. The heady mixture stronger than wine, and just as intoxicating.

Her body reacted, the ache settling low, and heat flared between her legs. Even as she closed them tight, there was a persistent throbbing there.

"Is this some kind of madness?" She whispered the question which remained unanswered.

Her thoughts turned to the book she'd seen in Elspeth and Aeddan's cabin once more. The illustrations of the man and the women engaged in congress. "Is this what it's like?" Would being with him soothe the need that grew and grew inside her? Would the storm calm and settle?

She whipped back the sheets and rose, opened the window, and welcomed the cold air. Her body reacting to it, a wicked gust blew, and it brushed over the delicate material of her bedgown, teasing at her nipples, and she gasped, shutting the window as the door to her chamber opened.

"Miss? You dress now for the wharf?" Mei slid inside the room and shut the door with a click.

"No. I have no errands to run." She bustled to the small table, drew close a slip of paper, and scribbled a note. She considered it, then screwed it up and tried again, this time emboldened by the realization that it wasn't a conversation one could undertake via letter. Her sister would be scandalized, but she had to strike now, while there was still time.

Langdon,
I must see you. I remain at home today but need to talk with you.
Please, we will be at home to visitors from two in the afternoon.
Isabelle

It went against every rule of propriety, but she wanted to know passion far more than spending her later years a spinster wishing she'd tasted pleasure once in her life.

She sealed it and wrote a direction on the face of the paper then shoved it at Mei. "Have one of the boys deliver this immediately. Then return here as I wish to bathe and dress."

The girl took the message with a bow, then withdrew as Isabelle stalked to the closet and flung it open.

"What to wear?" The importance of seeing him and feeling confident and beautiful in the circumstances couldn't be overstated.

Day gowns and walking gowns vied for attention as she turned from the evening and ball gowns. At the end of the row sat an ensemble she'd not yet worn—mossy green with a seafoam inlay of silk. The exquisite lace collar and detail were more than merely charming. Matching boots sat on a shelf, and she sighed her satisfaction.

"This one will be perfect." Next, she considered the accessories she'd require.

Mei returned, and a bath was delivered to the center of the room by the two footmen, piping hot water added by two more housemaids, and finally, once the room settled again, a screen moved into place in front of the door. Divested of her gown, Isabelle wrapped a cloth around her hair, not wanting to wet it and attend to the drying, even though the fireplace emitted a wall of heat. She sank gratefully into the water. The lavender soap washed away any ounce of grime or odor until she was sure her skin shone. Rising, Mei wound the towel around her, and she stepped from the water.

"The green silk day dress, Mei. At the back of the closet," she instructed.

The girl retrieved it and laid it over the bed together with the underwear while Isabelle unwound her locks from the towel.

Stepping into the delicate underthings, she wondered what Langdon would think could he see her. Her mind tried to create an idea of what he'd look like dressed in his underthings, but it was impossible. How could she imagine what she guessed to be perfection?

Wrenching her thoughts back to reality, she stepped into the gown and set about fastening the many buttons at the front of the bodice while Mei was attending to the fastening of the skirt. Now she stepped into the delicate shoes and took her place at the toilette table. Mei moved in behind her, brushing and looping her hair, pinning it then adding a small posy of hothouse blooms.

"Miss looks most beautiful."

Isabelle smiled. "Thank you, Mei. I couldn't have done it without you." She rose and headed for the door, then turned back. "You are a treasure, Mei."

*L*angdon stared at the message on the salver. "When did this arrive, Fuchs?"

"Only in the last few minutes, sir."

He reached out, and the subtle scent of vanilla filled him. "Isabelle." He broke the seal and scanned the contents, a frown forming. "What could she want?"

For a moment, he nearly considered she was asking for more... A fuller experience than they'd enjoyed the night before. *Don't be a fool, man. She's a lady in most senses of the word.* She was gently reared. She wouldn't be asking for intimacies. And he highly doubt, even if she did, it would be without the commitment of a gold band.

Still, the thought remained, and his anatomy reacted.

He considered what he'd planned to wear, then discarded it. "Not this one, Fuchs," he grunted. "The gray stripe."

Fuchs raised his bushy, white brows then bowed deeply. "Of course." He hurried to retrieve it from the dressing room. When he returned, he also carried a fresh shirt, cravat, and boots. "These too, I think?"

Langdon opened his mouth, the customary remonstration dying away. "Yes, of course."

Fuchs laid out the clothing as Langdon lowered himself into the chair and waited for the man to shave him. His man applied the hot towel, and he allowed himself to relax. The slide of the razor over his skin was gentle and sure. It was one of the few things he'd missed during his time with the army, and when his service was done, Fuchs had once more attended to his needs as a valet.

With the shave completed, he took the damp cloth offered, wiped away any traces of cream from his skin, and completed his daily ablutions before he could dress. Fuchs assisted him into his clothes, straightening his ascot necktie so it sat just right.

"Will you wish to dine here tonight? Cook is hopeful of a

night off, and you're the last person I believe to respond to his request."

"I... No. I'm attending something or other——" "Mrs. Basingdon's soiree, I believe."

"I'll dine at the club then, I think." He reached for the other notes in the salver. One was from Justina, and he frowned, cracking the wafer.

My dear Langdon,
Forgive my contact, but I have no wish to accept the full amount,
yet the bank will not allow me to return the balance. I would
appreciate your assistance in settling this matter.
Yours respectfully,
Justina Elgin

Langdon grimaced. He didn't want the damned money back. He knew her financial situation, and accepting even a small portion of the funds, he knew, sat poorly with the woman. But he'd wanted to help. If only in such a small way.

"Fuchs, one moment." He settled at the small escritoire and considered how to answer.

Justina,
I require no repayment. The funds are to assist you from one
friend to another. If you wish, whatever remains could perhaps be
donated to a charitable organization in your name. Above all,
though, make use of whatever will allow you to fund your chil-
dren's education and your return home.
With the greatest regards, L

"Have this delivered to Mrs. Elgin forthwith. When I return, have my clothes ready for tonight's events, then you are excused for the rest of the evening."

"If you're sure, sir?" Fuchs peered at him, harrumphed,

then continued. "Then I'll make the arrangements you require and will see you tonight."

Langdon left the room on a jaunty step.

He'd just cleared the stoop when a man stepped up to him. "Sir, if I might have a word?" Stubens, one of the men he'd directed to investigate Forster Shipping, had clearly been waiting for him. He looked respectable enough if rumpled and wearing ill-fitting clothing.

Landon scanned the street, then grunted, "This way." He turned the corner and ducked down the side alley. "If you're going to come to this section of town, you should wear a suit."

"Huh?" the man said, looking down. "I've been up all night, Major, and I haven't had a chance to dress properly yet."

It might very well be, considered Langdon, but the creases offended his sensibilities, being used to pristine army uniforms his batman had pressed with regularity. Then he sighed and mentally shrugged off the thoughts. "What?"

"Miss Forster? She's on the up-and-up. I got into the office and checked what she's been doing as you requested. Cargo, staffing, and updating manifests as would be expected. She's also inspected the building and routines and demanded changes. But as far as I can see, she hasn't got anything to do with transporting contraband."

Landon huffed out a deep breath. Relief coursed through his veins, and that was something he didn't want to consider too deeply.

Stubens scratched his head then shrugged. "But there's been some oddities. It seems three cartons appeared on the dock when the *Jackson* set sail and weren't accounted for. The right amount of cargo was dispatched, but these crates contain items on the manifest, yet they are not the correctly numbered items. Don't know what went out instead. She investigated but found nothing to tell her what was in the replacement crates."

The words chilled his gut. "What did she discover from the investigation?"

Stubens sighed. "There was a mix-up at the port. Three crates meant for another line were loaded onto the *Jackson*, and the three which don't appear to marry up with those listed for shipping. They were moved into the warehouse. Miss Forster wasn't happy and talked to the men, but they did the clammy-clam and admitted to nothing. No one else seems to know anything either."

Landon tapped his cane on the ground as he considered the situation. "Keep an eye out. Continue your inquiries, but be discreet. Have one of your men follow Miss Forster when she travels, but keep them out of sight. If there's any danger, they're to protect her at all costs."

The man searched Langdon's face then nodded. "Yes, sir." Stubens peeled away, melting into the alley behind Langdon, who stepped forward, checked to ensure no one saw him, and stepped into the street.

It all smelled like a set-up of some kind. But what could it be? The questions piled up without any answers.

Isabelle fidgeted, unable to settle to a task. The bookwork that would usually interest her lay unaddressed. She could perhaps take up needlework, but she despised it.

She stood, marched to the window, and peered out.

"Is something amiss?" Elspeth spoke quietly, and Isabelle closed her eyes, furious she'd been unable to contain herself.

"Why should there be?" If she worked hard and turned away from Elspeth, she might be able to fool her sister into thinking it was really nothing.

"Because you haven't settled since you came downstairs.

Isabelle? Please talk to me." Elspeth's beseeching tone echoed in the room. "Or is it someone?"

Isabelle whirled. "How did you know Aeddan was the man you wanted to be with?"

Elspeth's eyes widened. "So, the major?" She cocked her head. "Is that it?"

Biting her lip, Isabelle averted her gaze as she considered how to answer. "We leave in under ten days, yet I want something. I can't describe it, Elspeth." Tears burned in her eyes as she considered the question thoroughly.

She was saved from answering further as the doors opened and in came Lady Hawkston and her unmarried daughter, Charlotte.

Retreating to her wing chair, Isabelle lowered herself in it and accepted the role of unmarried sister, pouring tea and making small talk with the much younger lady, who prattled about hair and balls, gowns, and dashing men. It was akin to the scratching of fingernails on a slate blackboard.

Others came and went, the hour of three approaching when Major Deveraux was announced. Several of the ladies twittered as he entered, one going so far as to comment, "Oh, he's so eligible. If only I could catch his attention."

That had Isabelle curling her fingers as she reined in the sudden flash of jealousy.

His gaze captured hers, dark and promising, and thoughts of last night's kiss warmed her deep inside. Curiously melting her.

He made small talk with Elspeth and waited with an impatient air as the current crop of visitors made their departure.

Elspeth rose and cleared her throat. "If you'll excuse me, I must talk to the housekeeper about a matter of great importance. Perhaps you would like to take a turn in the gardens while I attend to this?"

Isabelle nearly gasped at the inappropriate behavior

Elspeth was allowing, then captured a glimpse of the twinkle in her sister's eyes. *She's excusing herself to allow us time alone.*

Isabelle scooped up the thick shawl she'd brought downstairs, hopeful for a quiet opportunity to speak, even if it were outside. "There's a greenhouse too," she rambled. "I'm sure you'd like to see it. Within are oranges and lemons and—"

"Show me the way, Miss Forster." His voice flowed over her, deep and dark. Full of something she thought could be promising.

Isabelle tugged the shawl around herself against the cold and led the way out the door and down a set of steps. The flags beneath their feet echoed as she headed to the greenhouse, the contents hidden by lush palms within the glass and metal structure.

He opened the door, and she stepped inside, the scent of earth redolent as the door closed with a barely audible click. They ventured deep within the greenery and there, in the center, sat a small chair, and she sank into it. Isabelle's stomach quivered, her hands shaking as she held tightly to the woolen accessory.

He settled into the single chair opposite. "You wished to talk privately?"

Where do I begin? Fear and excitement warred. "Last night..." she choked out, then wondered if this was the silliest thing she'd ever done in her life.

"Last night," he urged.

She glanced away, swallowing the lump that suddenly filled her throat.

She felt his presence as he shifted, the crinkle of material loud in the silence. The heat of him surrounding her. The smell of him enveloping her senses. When his fingers caught her jaw and turned her to face him, everything inside melted just a little further.

Langdon stared deeply into her eyes. "I want you, Isabelle. I want to love you."

Her eyes widened. She felt them as surely as her mouth opened.

Leaning a little closer, the whisper of his breath caressed her lips. "I want you naked so I can caress every inch of luscious skin."

Sanity raised its head in the middle of his stirring speech. "But..."

"You feel it too, don't you, Isabelle." It was not a question but a statement of fact. "This pull between us. The desire that pulses in the heart of your veins."

Cupping her cheek, he pulled her inexorably closer. Their lips touched, and it felt like the caress of a butterfly wing. The tiny flames that had licked at her insides since last night rose, fanned by the words, the touch, and the scents.

Just beyond, wind rattled the doors so they shuddered with a loud thud. It tugged them both back to reality which impinged. "We shouldn't be here," she said.

"Mrs. Fitzsimmons knows we're here. Remember? She suggested a walk," Langdon added.

"Countess," she muttered without thought then blinked. "Oh, blast!" She'd just given away her brother-in-law and sister's status. *They asked me not to tell!*

Langdon blinked. "Hmm. Yes, I did wonder when I heard his name." His lips widened into a wolfish smile. "I won't tell if you don't."

She twisted her fingers in her lap, taking a giant leap of faith. "I want to know about pleasure, but we leave in ten days."

"What?" He shot up out of the seat. "Leave?" he repeated, his face betraying his surprise. "I knew Fitzsimmons and your sister..."

"Uh, yes." Her mind struggled to process; he was more surprised with her announcement of their departure than her rash and highly improper request.

"No. You have to stay." His face tightened. "I'll discuss this with the...Mr. Fitzsimmons immediately." Langdon reached down and tugged her up. "If you leave, we won't get to the bottom of my mission."

This time it was Isabelle who blinked. "Mission?"

"Yes," he bit out, as if he'd come to some unpalatable realization in the split second since she'd announced they were leaving until now. "I'm here working for the government."

"Oh."

He tugged her after him, and she felt like the wake of a ship. Lost and at the mercy of the sea heading for the door.

"Well, I'm sure that explains many things." Isabelle blinked, trying to work out how everything fit together.

"Damn it." He dragged a hand through his hair, disordering it. "I shouldn't have told you that."

"Indeed." Cold settled in her belly. "So that's what this is about?" She bit her lip, controlling the sudden, intense pain.

"No. You and I are different. But it's all connected." He turned away, shook his head, then spun back, reached for and grabbed her hand.

They moved through the greenhouse and out into the cold, across the flags and back to the rear door. He stopped, whirled, and tugged her close. Their lips crashed together, mouths opening, and the taste of him intoxicated her.

"You have to stay, Isabelle. Because I crave you more than completing my mission."

His words stripped of polite-society-polished-shine scored her brain. Drove in and settled deep in her psyche.

"I don't want to go," she whispered.

"Then don't."

"I have to. I can't stay as an unaccompanied and unmarried woman. Already I'm considered unnatural for my daily visits to the warehouse and—"

"Then stay. With me."

She sucked in a sudden and unsteady breath. "No!"

Isabelle backed away from the suggestion of being little more than a courtesan.

"As my wife."

Everything changed in that second. "Wife?"

"Yes. Marry me. You've got more spine than most women I've ever met. We have a connection, which, if I'm not mistaken, will grow. You're a lady, and I must marry." He babbled, the words sounding like he was encouraging himself as much as her.

"I..."

"Yes. Say the word, Isabelle."

"Yes," she parroted.

"Good. Let's go talk to Mr. Fitzsimmons."

Langdon entered the library where he'd previously held discussions with Fitzsimmons.

His mind whirled while he gripped tight to Isabelle's hand. He'd had no intention of proposing marriage until she'd told him they were due to leave within days.

Urgency coursed as he faced the man looking up from the massive wooden desk at him. "Major Deveraux." Fitzsimmons's gaze fell to where Langdon and Isabelle's hands twined together.

"I intend to marry Miss Forster. She's agreed." He forced the words out, his stomach a mass of knots.

Fitzsimmons's face darkened. "Isabelle, have you agreed without coercion?"

"Yes, Aeddan." She spoke clearly, and her brother-in-law turned to gaze upon her pale but set face. "I wish to marry him and remain here."

Triumph roared in Langdon's chest, and he turned back to the man watching them both. "Why?"

He waited for Fitzsimmons to expand on the question. He

may very well be asking permission, but he refused to be treated like a green boy.

"Isabelle, would you attend Elspeth? She's in the parlor at the back of the house. I want to discuss things with the major."

"But—"

"Please," urged Fitzsimmons, cutting her argument short.

Langdon heard her leave, the swish of her gown, the closing of the door.

"Sit down, Major, and explain why the sudden desire to marry my sister."

He settled into the seat, the heat from the fire leaving his skin prickling. "There are many reasons. I can give you the 'I wish to marry her because she's beautiful and meets all my family requirements', but it's more than that."

"The Earl of Ravenhelm?" Fitzsimons's face wreathed in smiles, assured he'd surprised Langdon.

"Well, yes, Fitzsimmons. But then again, no less so than your family. I assume that's Carrington if I know my peerage."

"Ha! So, what are you here to achieve?" Fitzsimmons steepled his fingers.

"The government wishes to stop the import of opium into China, but there are covert sources at work. We believed Forster Shipping was involved. Not at the level of the ladies. More likely they are being used as unwitting carriers for contraband of many kinds."

Fitzsimmons nodded. "There are couriers in some crews I believe, but not Forster Shipping. They do act for the crown on occasion, the captains themselves acting as carriers, but I sincerely doubt any man working for Forster would do the same for our enemies. However, I did learn other ships were used for such tasks, unfortunately. I came across information concerning that while in India."

"Then you understand the dangers, Fitzsimmons. As my

wife, Isabelle would have to face the truth that she too may be targeted." Langdon's foot itched, as it always did in fraught situations. He'd learned to both respect and control it as necessary.

The man seated opposite nodded. "I do. That's why I have reservations about your marriage to Isabelle. She's not as strong as you may think. Malaria nearly killed her. After my experiences in India, where the danger was extreme, it was only Elspeth's quick reflexes that saved her. Isabelle is far more delicate."

"Perhaps she is, and perhaps she isn't. But she's a woman. Capable, beautiful, and of age, Fitzsimmons. I wish to marry her. She wishes to marry me. This today, is more a courtesy."

"Not because of her fortune, is it?"

Langdon's hackles rose, but he contained the rage that burned deep inside his gut. His fingers may curl, but he'd be damned if he'd show the revulsion he felt. "I do not need her funds. In fact, I'd rather have nothing to do with them and am happy to sequester her connection to Forster within a marriage contract."

Fitzsimmons subsided with a smile, and Langdon had the thought he'd somehow passed a test.

"Very good. You're right, of course, she is of age, and it is ultimately her decision, but I had to be sure. I care for her as I do any of my sisters. Now, let's focus on your mission. Tell me more."

Chapter Eight

ISABELLE WAITED. The hastily assembled finery of heavy silk in tones of cream and green floated over her narrow waist and captured at the back in a fountained bustle.

Her hair was caught up under her hairpiece, perched high on her head, of the same cream and green tones as her gown, the veil a filmy mask of lace that she presently flicked over the top of the hairpiece. She would drop it down once they entered the chapel.

"You look beautiful, Isabelle," breathed Elspeth.

Tomorrow her sister and Aeddan would leave, and she'd remain with a husband she barely knew—though her body yearned for him—in a country that was utterly alien to her. It's perfectly acceptable to feel a moment of disquiet, she told herself.

Aeddan and Elspeth had both urged them to take over the lease on the house, given it was more suitable than the rooms Langdon had resided in. His man, Fuchs, would arrive this evening, and somehow it felt odd to be in this position, considering assuming the role of the woman of the house.

In the last week, she and Elspeth had set about arranging Elspeth's trunks, finding gowns, and attending fittings for

Isabelle's trousseau and Elspeth's newly fitted gowns that would expand with her waistline. There'd been arrangements concerning her affairs, and most notably the marriage contract ensuring her funds were entrusted for any children they might produce.

She'd barely even seen Langdon, except when he called with a ring to celebrate their engagement, and to sign the documents. Other than that, he'd been curiously absent.

The door to the bedroom opened. She knew the footsteps, muffled though they were by the deep pile of the carpet. Mei, carrying items into the room in readiness for later.

"You're sure, aren't you?" Elspeth spoke quietly, breaking the insular thoughts Isabelle had sunk into.

Was she sure? She didn't know him, but she wanted him so much. She wanted to learn about passion. If they'd had time, the period of 'getting to know you' most couples enjoyed, maybe there wouldn't be this tiny bit of fear.

"Isabelle?"

Now she turned, pasting a smile onto her face, needing Elspeth to believe the fiction she was about to share. "Of course. He's charming and well-positioned. An earl's son. I will be very happy. I have no doubt."

Elspeth nodded slowly. "I have something. Aeddan and I were gifted this before we left India, but I think it may be..." She broke off and blushed a deep rose. "You'll see. Don't open it now though." Elspeth handed her a package wrapped in brown paper and tied with string.

A book. Suddenly, knowledge speared Isabelle. Elspeth had given her the book wrapped in purple silk. The one containing the illustrations.

"I—"

"Later." Elspeth stilled her as she rose up. "We should go down in a moment, but first, you know of certain expectations?"

Isabelle reached over and took Elspeth's hands. "I do. I'll

be fine, my dearest." With a nod, she looked to the door. "They'll be waiting."

Elspeth sighed then led the way, her matronly blue gown swishing as she walked, and Isabelle took up the small posy of silk flowers Langdon had sent her just this morning. A mix of iris, peony, and chrysanthemum.

"You have received flowers, Miss Isabelle. You should carry today."

She blinked, rising from the bed as she pulled the wrap around herself. "What? Where?" Mei extended the bouquet for her to inspect.

"They're beautiful."

"Auspicious," added Mei with a smile. "Each flower has a meaning. He sent you iris to keep the evil spirits at bay, peony for wealth, beauty, and long life, and chrysanthemum for love over a long life."

"I... How do you know what they mean, Mei?"

Mei handed her the cup of tea, and she sipped slowly, considering the girl before her. "It is known they bring good luck, Miss Isabelle. My mother taught me."

They walked to the carriage, Aeddan assisting Elspeth in then helping Isabelle up before sitting opposite her in the carriage. "You look beautiful, Isabelle," he murmured against her cheek.

"Thank you," she whispered because suddenly this all felt real. Her life was changing, and she'd no longer be the unmarried sister. Instead, she'd have a new life—a different persona.

Nothing would ever be the same again.

It wasn't bad, just scary, Isabelle reminded herself. An adventure of the kind she'd never envisaged but desperately wanted. It was within her grasp.

They rattled along until they reached the Holy Trinity Cathedral, and she drew in a deep and surprisingly unsteady breath. Before she could move, Aeddan stopped her. "You're sure?"

"Yes, Aeddan."

He nodded, though his gaze settled a moment longer before they moved, and Aeddan helped both of the women from the carriage then tucked her arm in his as they entered the great hall.

In the end waited Langdon, Fuchs, Mei, and even Mrs. Hargraves. They moved in slow, measured steps, her nerves melting away as she slid the veil over her face. Langdon turned his smile her direction.

Finally, she stood beside him. The Bishop talked. Isabelle wasn't sure what he said or asked. She must have answered his questions because Langdon was sliding the ring onto her finger.

He turned her, and they kissed once he'd raised the veil. It seemed only a moment later they signed the register that made their union official. Cries of "hurrah" filled the air, but they came from so far away. Her awareness settled on the weight on her hand. The feel of his arm around her, and the knowledge that they were now man and wife, almost over-whelmed Isabelle.

"Come, wife." He urged her down the aisle, and once they stepped into the light, after the dimness within, she blinked.

A second carriage waited, decorated with flowers and ribbons. Langdon handed her in before turning to Aeddan and Elspeth. "We'll meet you at the house."

He climbed in then reached for her, and the carriage moved on, the clop of the horse's hooves loud. Langdon reached over and untied the strings of her bonnet.

"What are you doing?" Her voice sounded breathless.

The smile he gave was naughty. "I'm replacing it with this." He indicated to a small box on the seat beside him and lifted the lid to reveal a circlet of flowers. "Lilies symbolize a happy union for a hundred years, and orchid for wealth, fortune...and love."

Langdon leaned over, placing the floral tribute on her head before kissing her. The passion between them exploded, and he tugged her close, so she felt the rapid beat of his heart through the many layers of clothing.

When he tugged away, they both panted. "Tonight," he whispered, the words a promise of passion and so much more.

The carriage rounded the corner and entered the drive, coming to a stop outside the house. Nothing had changed. Except herself, she thought dazedly. This time when she climbed down, it was as a married woman. The rattle of a second carriage captured Isabelle's attention, and with her arm tucked safely into Langdon's, she turned and watched as Aeddan and Elspeth's carriage filled the spot theirs had vacated.

The pair descended the carriage and joined them. "You should go inside, so as not to catch your death," cajoled Elspeth.

Aeddan smiled and ushered his wife inside without a word.

Isabelle made to turn when Langdon swooped, picking her up and carrying her inside and over the threshold. "What?" she squeaked.

"Avoiding any bad luck." He laughed, joined by Aeddan once they were inside.

She blushed hot and red as he placed her down on the floor. "Really." Isabelle set about straightening her skirts, hoping it would mask just how flustered she felt. Then, sure her flower crown would slip, she raised a hand to steady it in place.

"What a pretty circlet, but where's your bonnet?"

Isabelle turned to Elspeth. "In the carriage."

Elspeth smiled. "I'll have Jacinthe bring it inside."

One of the housemaids appeared and accepted their outer garments, and Elspeth disappeared to give directions for the meal, then they made their way into the dining room for the bridal lunch.

The room was festooned with flowers, the table set for the four of them with shining crystal and silver, not to mention snowy white linen. Once they'd settled into the seats, a feast was brought forward. Syllabub and game, jellies and even tropical fruits rounded the meal. The champagne she'd had no idea had been laid in tickled her nose, and by the end, she was feeling relaxed.

Elspeth and Aeddan retired, but it was as if she didn't notice, her entire focus on Langdon.

"Come with me, wife."

The words ignited the slow burn deep inside, and she took his hand.

*L*angdon led Isabelle up the stairs, and once they reached her chamber, he stopped. The kiss he pressed upon her was soft. Teasing with a hint of promise. "I'll join you soon."

Isabelle stood there, fingers pressed to her lips, her gaze following his every move as he stepped back, bowed deeply, and retreated down the hall to the room he'd agreed to use for the evening.

His body hardened with sexual hunger, and he wondered how on earth he'd be able to contain himself this evening. He'd need to use everything he'd ever learned of pleasure so he didn't frighten or cause her any fear of the marriage bed.

Fuchs waited, a deep steaming bath at the ready. "May I offer my congratulations, sir?"

"Thank you, Fuchs. Has Mei arrived to attend my wife?"

"Yes, sir. I handed her the parcel myself and gave instructions as to the preparation of her chamber. There will be hot water waiting and the items of apparel ready."

Langdon smiled. Tonight he would introduce his wife to passion. And he would ensure she enjoyed every moment of it.

Chapter Nine

____

ENTERING ISABELLE'S chamber was like stepping into an alien world. Where previously it was lovely, though a little cloying with the green and gold coverings, now it flickered with firelight. Scented candles of rose and lily filled the air, the fire flickered in the corner, and a screen of wood and silk, artfully decorated with bamboo, hid whatever was out of view.

Mei waited and ushered her around the corner. A steaming bath waited, and she smiled. "Thank you for your thoughtfulness."

The girl smiled. "The major requested it." Isabelle lifted her hands and removed the circlet, the young girl receiving it and placing it into a box. "You'll wish to keep, yes?"

"Yes."

Isabelle stripped, sighing as the weight of the gown was removed from her, then sank into the water once naked.

She closed her eyes and inhaled deeply, allowing her senses to float as the water lapped at her skin. Tiny blossoms danced on the surface of the lightly scented water, yet another facet to the attention he paid to her.

Honestly, for the first time, she noted how the caress of the water over her skin relaxed and yet fanned the heat which lay, banked within but ready to burst into flame when Langdon touched her. "That's how it feels," she murmured then cast her gaze toward Mei, who was busy opening a package on the chaise at the other side of the room, and her eyes drifted shut.

Movements from the other side of the screen intruded, and she opened her eyes.

Mei returned, a large bath-sheet in her hands. Isabelle rose and noted the way the water sluiced down her body.

The cloth enveloped her, and once more, the masses of sensations set her belly quivering. Mei returned with a wickedly ethereal gown of silk. "From the major."

"It's so light," she murmured, sliding into the pale cream, decorated with red and gold dragons—the nightwear so sheer it was as if she remained naked—and added the wrap. Far more delicate than the cambric gown she'd had made for tonight, she thought.

The material of the gown seemed to move in the firelight as she stepped around the screen.

Isabelle settled into the chaise while staff came and retrieved the bath, the screen granting her privacy as Mei brushed her hair.

The flickering of the candles, the scent all adding to the unreality of this night. A knock echoed on the door, then it opened. Langdon—her husband—stepped within. He nodded to Mei, and the girl bowed deeply, scooping up the last items littering the floor, and left the room.

Langdon advanced, and she noted the bottle in his hand. "You look relaxed, Isabelle." The lump she'd been so sure she'd overcome returned, and she nodded mutely.

His smile widened, and he glanced around the chamber, his gaze settling on a salver and the two glasses. "Come, take a glass with me."

Isabelle rose, her legs shaking with anticipation, and made her way over.

The cork popped, he poured two drinks and passed one to her, placing the bottle down then taking up his glass. "We should drink a toast, Isabelle."

"What..." she croaked and cleared her throat. "What should we drink to?"

"Us. To a long, happy, and fruitful life."

The fire inside her was echoed by those she caught sight of in his gaze. She lifted the glass and sipped, more than a little aware that the frisson of awareness between them grew thicker and more substantial.

"I'm not sure..." Her tongue had thickened, making it hard to speak.

"We've got all night."

Strangely, his words didn't soothe. *All night.*

He stalked toward her, long-legged strides reminding her of some kind of predator. Now, Isabelle's hand shook.

"You're not afraid, are you, Isabelle?"

God knew she wanted to put up a front of bravado, but the truth was she was all at sea. It wasn't terror, but the not knowing—

"I won't hurt you." He stopped opposite her and cupped her cheek tenderly with his hand.

"I want you to know pleasure. That's what you asked me for. It's what I'll give you." His voice dropped to a lower register, and the echo of his words ricocheted.

Isabelle stepped back and turned, sipping the champagne as she willed her crazed body to settle.

"Isabelle?"

"I want this," she whispered, "but I don't know how. I know the steps, but..." She broke off, not exactly sure what she wanted to tell him. Everything she'd heard from the maids was the basics, but she didn't recall any talk about the emotions like fear. There'd been plenty of lewd comments about want. That didn't come anywhere near to explain what she was feeling right now.

His hand curled over her shoulder, fingertips massaging gently. "We can sit and talk."

Under his urging, she moved to the chaise and sank down, grateful that he was tender enough to understand she was out of her depth.

"Control is important to you, isn't it?" He settled beside her, and she nodded, then turned to the front, so she wasn't facing him.

"We were young when Mama died. I was eleven and Elspeth thirteen. Since then, Elspeth and I shared the running of the household, even while we attended a local academy as day students, caring for Louisa and Papa until he died. My aunts stepped in for sometime when we finished our schooling, forbidding us to travel because it was unseemly. Our father was adamant we needed to learn the business, to take over when the time came, then we assumed the daily running of Forster Shipping. It's what I do best. Elspeth is more attuned to dealing with traders and choosing cargo." Closing her eyes, Isabelle concentrated on breathing, taking oxygen in and out, while she calmed her nerves, her hand on her chest like it could soothe the race of her heart. "I'm not missish, Langdon. I'm not incapable of making decisions, but order is important to me. Precedents and so on allow me to run the line efficiently."

"No, you're not missish at all, Isabelle. You're direct and forthright. Capable. Tonight is something different though. There are no rules except the ones we make. Together."

Langdon's words centered on her. They made sense, and for the first time since he'd entered the room, she could breathe freely again.

"Langdon? Will you... Please, kiss me." Now she turned, hoping he'd read in her eyes that she was ready to try.

The smile on his face warmed. He reached over, cupping her cheek once more, and brushed a thumb over her lips, and the nerves quivered in response.

"Such beautiful lips. Rosy pink and lush." With each word, the whisper of his breath caressed her skin, her eyes drooping as he loomed closer.

The touch was soft, a butterfly wing. Her lips parted, welcoming him in memory of the scorching contact they'd already shared.

When the kiss deepened, she moaned. The fire in her belly was fanning out, so it invaded every point of her body.

Langdon's hand slid down to her shoulder, bringing her closer. Just enough so their bodies touched, then he pulled away. "Let me take that for you." He retrieved the glass from her loose grasp and set them on the small table beside the chaise. "Now, let's resume making our rules, shall we?"

His hands circled her waist and pulled her, so she half-loomed over him as their lips touched again.

This time Isabelle reached out and slid her hands onto his shoulders, finding the lapels of his dressing gown. She held tight to the soft material as he plundered, tongue and lips working their magic until she was sure she'd expire.

The sensation of tugging roused her as he slid one hand under the shoulder of her wrap so it fell away as she levered up a little. When she caught sight of the glint in his eye, she wondered if it was mirrored in her own, because her body wanted things she wasn't sure of. What she did know was she yearned for his touch.

Between her legs, an insistent pulse had started, and she squeezed them together, yet the action left her moaning.

He'd caught sight and smiled.

"Come, wife," he murmured and pulled her upright with him.

With a grin, he took her hand. Langdon reached for the belt of his gown and urged her to unfasten the knot. She fumbled a little, excitement sending zings of awareness through her veins. It gave, and the gown gaped.

Miles of flesh, bronzed chest, and God help her, his erection stood hard to attention.

She glanced up.

"Let me help you." With gentle fingers, Langdon slid the other arm of her wrap free so it slipped to the floor. "Let me help you with the fasteners, Isabelle." The tiny material frogs holding her nightgown together slid free without effort, and soon her gown too gaped. His face took on a hard slant, and he breathed faster.

"Langdon?"

"Rules, Isabelle," he muttered, and this time she reached first, her fingers grazing carefully over one pectoral muscle. It flexed at her touch.

"You like that, Langdon?"

"Very much." He slid the material of her gown over her shoulders. "Now, help me." Isabelle felt the shake of her legs as she reached up, pulled the lapels further apart, and with a gentle move, slid the material from his shoulders.

Now they stood, naked in the firelight.

"So beautiful," he rasped. "The same pink as your lips. Beautiful breasts," he whispered, and he reached out, sliding his hand under one so it plumped. His thumb sliding over the nipple. "Ooooh." It was like the ripple of sensation zinged down to between her legs.

"Langdon?"

"Just feel, *ma belle*." He bent forward, and to her surprise, his dark locks filled her gaze as he took the tip in his mouth. Tongue caressing and flicking while his other hand slid down to stroke her belly. He stepped away, eyes hooded, and reached out a hand to her. "Come with me."

The touch of his fingers as they closed around hers was warm. She followed him to the bed, surrounded by scented candles.

"This is our room, this place where the two of us can be ourselves. This is our sanctuary, Isabelle. A place where we can give and take. Love and be loved. Fulfill our wants and innermost desires." He kissed her collarbone with each statement, holding her close, so she felt every dip and hollow of his body.

His erection nudged at her, the scalding heat of him a surprise. Her own body was a stranger too—warm and swollen, and there was dampness between her legs. It was as if some secret part was waiting for a momentous event.

"Get on the bed, Isabelle." He turned, and she noted he reached for a bottle, the silver stopper gleaming in the light.

The silk bedcovers were puffed, and she sank into them. When Langdon turned, his hands were slick. "Let me prepare you."

The scent of jasmine filled the air as he joined her on the bed and reached for her arm. The oil he rubbed into her skin was warm, and every pass a wonder of care. Langdon took his time, sliding his hands over her skin firmly but gently up, ever upward until he reached her collarbone, and Isabelle watched. Mute.

"Jasmine has an exotic fragrance. It has long been used in perfumes, but even more, it's an essence of love. It increases intimacy and closeness. I hope that's what we'll build together."

Now his hands moved over her chest, heading for her breasts before he swooped down once more, fanning her nipples as he breathed. His tongue licked each erect nub, then he slid his thumbs over them.

"In some cultures, sexual congress is a way to attain spiritual enlightenment. It requires both lovers to give and receive, Isabelle. Is that what you want?"

Her mind splintering, she muttered, "Yes, Langdon. With you."

He continued his quest, and she grabbed his shoulders, holding on as her body betrayed the excitement that rode her.

"Your body is a temple. Perfect in every way."

Her belly quivered. His hands roamed over her skin, dipped into her navel then down to the curls that lay beneath.

"But even with the temple, there is always the sacred spot. The place where only the holiest can worship." He touched and opened her and sighed.

Isabelle glanced down to see his eyes closing as he touched her intimately.

"Ready for me. Damp. Hot." He slid a finger inside, just enough, and stilled. She cried out, overwhelmed by the sensations that crashed over her. Her fingers bit deep as she bowed off the bed, only dimly aware he'd pulled away enough to grasp her hips. "God help me, Isabelle, but I don't think I can wait. I need you." His voice sounded gravelly.

"Please, Langdon."

"What? What do you want, Isabelle? Tell me about your rules."

"Love me. Worship in the temple," she panted.

"Open your legs then."

She did, and he shifted, his body looming over hers. He swooped in now and kissed her, ragged and demanding, but she welcomed and returned it. Hard. Lips and tongue parried.

He lowered himself. "Feel me." He took her hand, pulled it toward himself so she could run her fingers down his length. "I'm going to worship you with this. Inside. Deep."

She shook again, this time pleasure and hunger demanding more.

Once again, he let go, opened her, fingers widening the intimate folds so she could welcome him inside her body.

He nudged. Hard. Hot. So swollen and demanding.

His hips flexed. Her breath fled.

He slid in just a bit. She burned and wriggled, but he pushed harder until he broke the barrier of her maidenhood. She screamed. He caught her mouth, taking in the sound.

Her body shook, the pain rippling, and she felt the sting of tears.

"Langdon?" Her voice wavered.

"Only the first time, Isabelle." He held himself tight, and his words were harsh. She could feel the shudders wracking his body, but he didn't move.

"Stop," she whimpered.

"This is the worst. It will pass quickly. I promise, *ma belle*." He held himself within her, the tension surrounding them. He flexed. She hissed and waited for more pain.

Nothing.

Again, he moved, and this time, it was free of the burn and tearing sensation.

"Can you feel me, Isabelle? Do you feel me worshiping you?" his lips whispered against her ear.

"I..." She struggled to concentrate now; the pleasure drugged her, veiling her senses as she sought to form an answer.

"Feel how I move deep inside your body. Know that from now on, there will only ever be pleasure between us." His hands gripped her buttocks, pushing deeper and further inside her. "When you're ready, I can show you many ways of pleasure, Isabelle. Ways of loving each other."

She moaned in his arms, lost in the waves of sensuality. "Yes, Langdon. Show me."

His mouth settled on her throat, and she arched again as he moved, involuntarily granting him everything.

Their moves came faster, wilder. Bodies moving with synchronicity. Finally, her body coiled tight, and she shattered in his arms.

He followed, pumping with a wild rhythm before stilling, holding himself deep within. Then he slumped down over her.

Chapter Ten

STARING AT THE CEILING, Langdon held Isabelle close against him. For a woman with no experience of lovemaking, she'd been more than willing to allow him the freedom of her body, and she'd responded. Shyly and without tutorage it was true, but he'd bet she'd become a tigress before long. He relished that knowledge.

His body was exhausted, but his mind whirred, unable to settle.

The last nine days had passed frantically. He'd arranged a special license, given up his rooms and moved into the house, arranged marriage contracts, and taken leave so he might enjoy a few days with his bride.

He'd also prepared a letter to send to his father. They weren't close, but his *pater* deserved to know that his son and heir had taken a wife.

Tomorrow, she would say goodbye to her sister and brother-in-law, who would leave on the *Venturer*. Isabelle would stay with a man she barely knew in a country she was an alien in. He remembered her words. *I'm not missish.*

No, she wasn't. At her heart, she was adventurous, courageous, and infinitely precious to him already. But there'd be danger. He'd already ensured Stubens's men would follow her once she resumed her work with Forster Shipping, but there were more significant issues at stake. Like the potential damage to his heart. He just hoped he could keep her safe, because losing her now was more than he could bear.

Flinging an arm over his eyes, he willed sleep to come.

*I*sabelle woke. Her body ached in strange ways, and she was warm if squashed. "What…"

The sound of a soft snore broke through the cloud of sleep. Snore. "Langdon?" she whispered and peered over the mound of bedcovers she didn't remember pulling over herself.

Bronzed skin. Naked, bronzed skin at that.

She glanced under the covers. Naked.

Her finger felt heavy. A wedding ring, her brain offered. Married.

She gulped as memories of the lovemaking the night before cascaded in her consciousness.

Carefully, Isabelle levered herself to the edge of the bed, searching for her wrap. She caught sight of mounded clothes by the chaise, and with a quick look, ensuring Langdon was still asleep, she scurried over, tugged on the first robe, and gave a squeak when she realized it was Langdon's.

"That suits you, *ma belle*." His sleep-roughened voice stilled her actions, and she whirled. "But I'd rather you took it off and came back here." He patted the bed.

"But you have your room and—"

He levered up in the bed. "Nothing between us should embarrass you, Isabelle." She stilled, once more at sea, dealing with new emotions, new feelings, and new situations. "I'm not sure how to react—"

"We set the rules. Our rules in our place. We start as we mean to live our lives."

Did that mean he planned to share a room with her? Her parents had, though she knew that was unusual within the highly born ranks. Aeddan and Elspeth did too. Then again, maybe Aeddan and Elspeth did so because they were in the colonies and aboard a ship.

What would be considered acceptable when she and Langdon returned to England? For that matter, did he even plan to return? So much she didn't know about him.

"When we return to England…" she blurted out.

He grimaced. "Our rules, Isabelle. Now come back here."

"One moment." She did need the bathroom and a few minutes to compose herself, and she scurried out of the room. When she returned, cups of tea had been delivered.

"Mei came in. I sent her off. Told her you'd ring when she was needed." Langdon was sitting up the in bed, his chest on display.

"You didn't look like that when she came in, did you?" Isabelle frowned. "I'm not sure she's used to seeing naked men."

"No, I slid under the covers before she could enter. Enough about Mei for now. Come here so I can bid you good morning properly."

Slipping into the bed with Langdon felt wicked and improper.

"You could take that off," he added slyly, and the put-upon look on his face left her smiling.

"I think I'll keep it on for now," she said as he leaned over, moving his lips over hers, and she melted all over again.

*L*angdon straightened his tie, once more thanking Fuchs for his planning. His wife remained in the bedchamber, her maid Mei preparing her hair. The rap of knuckles on the door startled him.

"Sir, Mrs. Fitzsimmons has indicated they will be ready to leave soon," Fuchs's voice called through the heavy door.

He opened it, glanced around, and noted that Isabelle now waited on the chaise, fully dressed.

Entering the chamber, he accepted the gloves his man passed, then waited as he fussed with the collar once more. This room didn't meet their needs, but once Isabelle's sister and brother-in-law vacated the house, he'd check the other places and they'd re-arrange to suit themselves.

"My dear, if you're ready?"

Isabelle stood and took his arm, and they headed for the door. When Langdon opened it, she gifted him with a broad smile of thanks as she preceded him out. He noted the sway of her hips, the narrowness of her waist, and he thanked fate for his luck.

They met Elspeth and Aeddan in the hallway. Elspeth looked pale and teary-eyed, while Aeddan shook his hand.

"We'll come with you down to the wharf," said Isabelle, and Langdon opened the door.

"Our trunks went ahead last night. Jacinthe and Grundy left once we'd dressed," babbled Elspeth, and Langdon understood the two women were very close; likely this was the first time they'd been apart since childhood.

Aeddan steered his wife from the house, and she moved slowly. For the first time, a glimmer of suspicion entered his brain in the devoted way the man attended his wife. He'd enquire with Isabelle later, Langdon thought.

The journey to the docks didn't take long, and soon, the sound of the wheels rolling over the wooden planks slowed.

They climbed from the carriage, and Langdon got his first look at the vessel that would carry the couple home. He handed Aeddan a letter. "You'll ensure this reaches my father?"

Aeddan smiled. "It will be much faster if I deliver it

myself. Look after Isabelle and yourself, and happy hunting. I have no doubt you'll find the culprits."

The men shook hands, and as Langdon turned to his wife, he noted the way the women embraced. Isabelle handing over a handkerchief and settling her older sister. It filled him with pride to see her so strong in what must surely be trying circumstances. Then Aeddan and Elspeth moved forward, up the gangplank, as the captain came forth to meet them.

Langdon moved to Isabelle, sliding her hand onto his arm. "They'll be fine. You told me the ship is one of your newer vessels."

Isabelle glanced at him. "Yes. It will shorten the journey by several weeks, depending on the currents and winds." She turned and gazed over the dockworkers completing the loading and frowned. "What are those crates doing there?" She indicated two that sat to the side, then strode forward.

"What? Isabelle, you should wait for—"

"No. See the numbers on the sides? They aren't ours."

She turned swiftly, heading for the warehouse when a bellow went up. "Watch out below!"

Langdon twisted, taking in the precarious sway of a crate on the hoist. Directly below, his wife made for the warehouse.

His gut twisted, and fear—such as he'd never before experienced—chilled him to the marrow. He broke into a run. "Isabelle!" He wouldn't reach her.

She'd be crushed under the weight of the contents.

What was probably a mere second or two in time took an eternity to pass.

From the corner of his eye, he caught sight of a burly man in stained clothes, face stark yet determined, racing toward his wife. The man grabbed Isabelle by the waist and hauled her some distance.

A crack echoed over the sudden silence.

The man launched out, and they flew through the air.

Isabelle and her rescuer landing on the planking, and Langdon heard her *oomph* as they hit the ground.

The crate fell to the floor with a crash.

Splinters flew, and the contents rolled—straw and china shards embedding themselves in any soft item within reach.

Right where Isabelle had been mere seconds before.

Time resumed its normal speed, and Langdon ran over and snatched her up and into his embrace. "Are you injured?"

She blinked once. Then again. Blue eyes wide with surprise. "No... I don't think so." With shaking hands, Langdon smoothed out her dress, looking for signs of injury. "I'm fine. Langdon, you can cease now." Her trembling voice broke through the fog enveloping his mind.

Closing his eyes, Langdon breathed deep, inhaling the scent of Isabelle and the soft, pliant form against his. Alive.

"Come, husband. We're making a scene. Come to the office." Isabelle took his arm and towed him to the office, picking her way through the shards.

They'd only just entered and settled into a chair when Aeddan crashed inside. "What the hell happened?"

Langdon looked over at the man, glowering at him. "I don't yet know, but I certainly intend to find out."

Aeddan rubbed a hand over his perspiring face. "Isabelle?"

"I'm unharmed, but you must return to the vessel, Aeddan. You need to be there for Elspeth. Just don't tell her what happened."

"I won't," Aeddan grunted then turned to spear Langdon with a sharp look. "Find whoever did this. Deal with it." With a last quick hug to Isabelle, Aeddan stalked from the building.

In the sudden silence, Langdon considered what he'd seen. "Who was the man on the dock?" he enquired, wondering how soon he could contact Stubens to find out what his men had seen even as he wondered if there was more to the scenario than he currently knew.

Isabelle screwed up her face. "I don't know. I'll check with Staindhouse when he comes inside."

It wasn't nearly enough, but for now, it would have to do. If only he could shelve his misgivings as quickly.

Isabelle understood Langdon's concerns. She had similar ones. Dangerous conditions on the wharf could not be tolerated, but there was also the issue of the now lost items and the two crates on the waterfront.

They waited until Staindhouse entered the building. "What happened out there, Staindhouse?" she demanded and stared at the man.

He blotted his face with a handkerchief. "I don't know, Miss Forster. But we will get to the bottom of it."

"Deveraux," Langdon corrected the man, who turned to look at her husband.

"Pardon me?"

"Mrs. Deveraux, Staindhouse. Who was the man on the dock?" Langdon bit out, and Isabelle sighed.

"Staindhouse, this is my husband. We were wed yesterday, so I am now Mrs. Deveraux.

However, who was the man on the dock who saved my life? I want to thank him." Staindhouse's gaze narrowed. "I don't know. I've never seen him before. Perhaps he's one of the crew of the vessel or——"

"The dock is unsecured?" Langdon's voice carried derision, and Isabelle reached out, patting his hand, understanding his concerns, but needing to make him understand.

"It's not like a barracks, Langdon. People come and go, delivering goods, collecting them, travelers, and crew access this area too." Isabelle spoke quietly, then turned to Staindhouse. "Please go see if you can find the man. I should like to thank him, but also, we should ensure he has sustained no injuries either."

Staindhouse left the office, and she stared at Langdon in silence. Her husband returned the gaze as moments ticked by. When the man returned, it was with a frown. "He's left, Miss... Uh, Mrs. Deveraux. No one knows him, where he came from, or why he was here."

She growled. "Have the men stay alert, and see what you can find out. I'm not staying today." Isabelle rose, shook out her skirts, and waited for Langdon to open the door. "I have retained the house. Any intelligence, please send it along to me there."

Chapter Eleven

LANGDON EXCUSED himself from the house late in the afternoon and headed for the small public tavern he knew Stubens often frequented.

Entering the dim taproom, he peered around, and he located the man at the end of the bar in a corner of the room. Langdon threaded his way through and was nearly upon Stubens when the man looked up. The young girl serving was called over, and Langdon ordered an ale. Not that he had any intention of drinking it, but he needed it to look as if he were there for a drink.

He settled onto the barstool beside his man and waited.

"Heard about the incident at the wharf this morning. My man, Fielding, was there looking around when he heard the ship's crane break. He saved Miss Forster."

"She's now my wife. And it's a damned good thing he did." Langdon still couldn't think about the incident without a chill coursing through his body.

"Yeah. He saw two men. They'd delivered the two crates sitting there when you arrived. I haven't had much opportunity to find out what else he saw or heard. I'm meeting him tonight here. And you shouldn't be. Don't want people to work out who's who as they say."

"No, I understand, but I want to know everything tomorrow. Meet outside the Oriental Bank at two. There's a laneway where we can talk."

"There'll be snow," the man added.

"You think?" countered Langdon.

"The sky is ominous enough. Send a message to my lodgings tonight with an alternative venue," Stubens muttered as another man pulled up beside him.

With no further opportunity to talk, Langdon carefully swapped tankards with Stubens then rose, leaving the taphouse.

Isabelle poured over the report Staindhouse had sent.

Mrs. Deveraux,

I have made inquiries concerning the man on the dock this morning. It appears he was looking for employment. However, after the incident, he left the docks. No one is currently aware of his whereabouts. I have asked the men to remain vigilant.
With regard to the ship's crane, we have ascertained this was a known issue. It was due to be attended to during the voyage. I met with the captain before he set sail, and he assured me this will be attended to forthwith.
The two crates on the dock are ours, I understand, and were loaded by hand. There have been no further incidents of unknown cargo being loaded to the best of my knowledge. I will continue my investigations concerning the previous episode, though based on my findings, I believe this to be an isolated incident.

Allow me to reiterate that the matter is now in hand, and I am infinitely grateful that no one, least of all yourself, was injured today.
I also wish to extend my felicitations on your marriage and wish yourself and the major a long and happy life.

Your humble servant,
M. Staindhouse Esq.

The door to her parlor opened, and Mrs. Hargraves entered the room. "Forgive me, Miss... Er, Mrs. Deveraux. But I've had the girls clean the rooms and wished to know when you were ready for us to relocate your things?"

Isabelle blinked. "Oh. I'd like to come upstairs and inspect first. I believe the major will be here soon, and no doubt his man will wish to make the arrangements for his items as well."

The housekeeper smiled. "Of course. If we're not interrupting then?"

Isabelle stood. "Not at all. I'll come now." She followed the woman from the room, and they headed up the stairs in silence.

Having never entered her sister or brother-in-law's rooms, she was more than interested to see their layout.

At what would be her room, she stopped and breathed deeply. Mrs. Hargraves opened the door, and Isabelle glanced within, seeing the pale floral tones she'd only once caught sight of— on the day of her arrival with Aeddan and Elspeth.

Entering the room, she noted the lush carpet of green with a small leaf motif. The walls, decorated with exquisite silk wallpaper, worked perfectly with the large bed, decorated with pale pink flowers on a cream brocade. The curtains were a perfect match, and the room was restful. Rather like the one she'd left behind in England.

Mrs. Hargraves opened a set of large white doors leading

to a dressing room and beyond that a bathing room. Another door, she was informed, led to the master's suite.

"Pray, open the door." Her voice might have sounded a little strangled, but she wanted to see the room that would house Langdon's items, and him too, should that be his choice. *I hope not.*

The room was also large and decorated with ruby bedding and curtains, the bathing room and dressing area almost identical to her own, but with more substantial fittings.

"Have Fuchs and Mei bring our things in, and instruct Fuchs should he wish to re-arrange at all to do so. I should also enjoy some fresh-cut flowers if that would be possible in my chamber."

She thought back over the night that had just passed. The scents of the candles had stimulated and enticed, and she wondered if that were only something done for their wedding night or... *Don't be forward, Isabelle.* But the question remained, chasing around in her brain like a dog after a rabbit.

Retreating to what would now become her room, she took in the chaise and small table. The boudoir chair, deep and lush, before the dressing table and the highly polished fireplace. Mei entered the room, carrying a parcel wrapped in brown paper and tied with string.

"Would you like me to open this, ma'am?"

Isabelle jerked. "No. Um, place it on the bed, and I will deal with it later." The parcel her sister had gifted them scored her mind. She wondered how Langdon would react to the contents. A knock echoed on the door, and Langdon peered inside.

"You're back already? When you said you needed to check on your work—"

"It was just a quick thing. What's that?" Langdon indicated to the parcel, and she felt the heat of a blush rising over her face.

"It's a gift from Elspeth and Aeddan."

He entered the room and reached for the package. "Not yet," she muttered. "Later. Once we've retired."

He looked at her, a question in his eyes.

"Later. It will be apparent then."

"All right. Tonight. Tell me, though, do you find the rooms comfortable?"

Isabelle blinked. "Oh, yes. I've inspected your room too and requested Fuchs to make any necessary adjustments to the layout and to unpack in there." Her stomach clenched a little, wondering if she'd overstepped. Those fears were quickly allayed when he nodded and smiled.

"Well then, we should leave them to it, as I have something I wish to discuss with you. Downstairs may be best." Langdon reached out, and she took his hand and followed him to the library. He shut the door behind him, and before she could move, he dragged her close.

Their lips met in a fiery kiss, and her mind blanked. It lasted forever to her beleaguered senses, yet it was over all too quickly. When they stepped back, they both panted, though he kept her circled by the band of his arms.

"Isabelle, I want you," he whispered against her neck, and memories of the night before, the intimacies, left her wracked with sensual hunger.

"It's daytime!"

He laughed at her embarrassment. "Our rules, *ma belle*. Daytime. Nighttime. Neither matters when it's you and I."

"Is it always so?" Isabelle wondered out loud then blushed deeply. "Oh, dear. Forgive me!"

"No, my dear. Not always. I've never..." He stopped, and a strange look came over his face. "No," he finished.

Isabelle wondered at his strange answer but pushed it aside. It probably wasn't a proper subject to discuss, she thought. She would need to work on proper, never having been all that concerned, but now that she was a married woman—a status she'd never expected to achieve—it would be important to abide by the unwritten rules.

"We should retire to the morning room," Isabelle suggested, and he quirked an eyebrow.

"Not just yet. I did want to discuss something with you." He disentangled himself and retreated to the desk, pulling a document from the drawer of the desk. "I need to tell you something. I spoke with Fitzsimmons before he left, and we agreed you should be aware."

Isabelle sank into a seat. "What?" She wondered about the sudden gravity of his words and the concern on his face.

"I am working with the municipal authority, it's true. I was placed there at the request of the government. The prime minister is wishful of stopping the importation of opium into China.

The emperor has made certain concessions available to the English. In light of that, the prime minister continues to seek those who import the contraband. We believe multiple shipping lines are being used covertly. At one point, there was a concern that Forster Shipping may be one targeted. There is also information smuggled out of China, likely to those trading in the drug. We have yet to track down who is passing the information."

She looked at him, dumbfounded. "So, you're a spy?"

He frowned. "Not really. More of a problem solver, Isabelle. But your arrival here has created some difficulties."

Now Isabelle leaned in. "What kind?"

"The incident on the docks? I don't believe it was an accident. You've been asking questions, investigating anomalies. It's odd that the crane broke at just that point. I've got people looking into things. They're also questioning the timing. From this point, if you must go down to the docks, either I accompany you or I will arrange an escort. For your safety."

Isabelle considered his request. The immediate reaction was to deny him, but he was concerned. It was only a small thing, and perhaps in giving that, there would be no issues with her continuation of running Forster Shipping.

"Very well," she agreed. "On the condition that you do not allow this escort to hamper my work. I will agree for now, but should you find that there is no involvement with Forster Shipping, then you will agree to remove my escort."

Langdon wanted to argue; it was there on his face in the way his lips tightened and his eyes narrowed. "Isabelle——"

"Promise me this, Langdon, and I will accept it."

"Damn it! Your safety is too important!"

Isabelle stood, the urgency of her request pushing her to make the point. "I need you to understand. The men must respect me. They must understand that I make the decisions and don't defer to you. Otherwise, I'm..." Isabelle sucked in a deep breath, casting her mind here and there for a way to explain. "If they see me deferring to you, they won't trust me. They won't take me or my direction seriously, and that puts Forster Shipping in a precarious position." She stepped closer, reaching out and taking the lead, cupping his cheek as he had numerous times hers. "I must be strong, Langdon. Please understand."

She closed the distance between them, setting her lips to his, opening them and licking his lips with a careful touch of her tongue, her eyes closing with the sudden knowledge of just how forward she was acting yet not caring.

The fragile relationship between them could be damaged if this agreement wasn't made. He might argue with the way she acted. If that were to happen, she'd be crushed.

Langdon groaned and opened to her, dominating and snatching control. His arms wound around her. One hand slid to her derriere, molding her abdomen to his and sinking the fingers of his other hand into her hair.

She moaned and squirmed. Her body was heating and firming, preparing itself for the ultimate expression of pleasure. She wanted him now with a burning hunger and so very much more besides.

Isabelle wanted not just passion but love. His love. The knowledge slammed into her as Langdon pushed her back. Her backside connected with the desk as their lips parted.

"I want to lift you onto the desk and push my way into you, Isabelle. You're not ready for that yet. That time will come. But know that I respect your acumen in business and always will. So, for now, I will accede to your requests." His voice ground, dark and enigmatic. "But be aware, I'm a man. I care for you, want nothing more than your safety, so while I may agree at this time, should the need arise, I will protect you. I will surround you if that's the only option to keep you safe."

Understanding the intent of his agreement, Isabelle nodded. "Very well."

His hand rose to her hair. "I've made a mess of your coiffure." Langdon tugged at pins, and her hair dropped around her shoulders.

"Langdon!"

"At home, wear it down for me. Please."

The heat in her belly banked. "At home." Now she smiled, feeling the jut of his erection.

"Our rules."

He smiled. "Yes. Our rules."

*L*angdon sealed the missive, satisfied that he'd done all he could to ensure Isabelle's safety.

Stubens would meet with himself and Isabelle in the morning. They would concoct a plan to ensure her safety during travel to and from the dock. The plan would also include the time she remained at the warehouse, but for now, he stood and placed his request on the salver. He stopped for a moment, noting the direction written in the black slashes.

Tonight they would make their first social appearance as a married couple. No doubt there would be surprise from the assembled persons. He'd been here a short time but had made no advances to any women of society, and certainly none that could lead to marriage, until Isabelle's arrival. She'd already changed him in many ways.

Hurrying up the stairs to his bedchamber, he had to fight the urge to enter her room. She'd be bathing, with miles of skin exposed. Langdon stopped and took a moment to suppress the constant hunger of his loins before opening his door.

Fuchs waited, the black evening suit laid out on the bed, his face betraying his relief at Langdon's arrival. "Thank heavens, sir. Now, if you'll bathe, we may have time to dress you before your wife is ready to depart."

Fuchs had been with him since his teenage years, so the tendencies to direct him didn't surprise. "I shall be swift, Fuchs. My ascot... It matches the color of my wife's gown?" Langdon had decided on a whim to surprise her.

"Uh, as closely as Mei and I could arrange, sir."

He smiled. "Excellent."

Langdon hurried to the bathroom, disrobing, and lowered himself to the water, wondering if perhaps he might entice his wife one day to join him in the deep and roomy tub. He washed quickly, then rose, dried, and headed back to the bedroom to dress.

Fuchs assisted him, and in short order, he once more appeared ready to squire the woman into society, thanks to Fuchs's fastidious assistance.

Langdon opened the door to her boudoir and entered. Isabelle was waiting as Mei slid a necklet against the skin of her throat, and he moved closer. "I will attend to that. Thank you, Mei."

His and Isabelle's gaze met in the mirror, his fingers sliding over her collarbone and stilling there. The rapid beat of her pulse warned him she was as vulnerable to the passion as he was.

Mei muttered something then left the room, and once more it was just the two of them.

"Your skin is soft, like silk. Your hair golden and shining in the firelight, and every time I'm near you, I want nothing more than to burn in the fire you ignite in me."

One of her hands covered his. He felt the quiver. "I have something I'd like to open with you before we leave, Langdon." She spoke in low, throaty tones.

His hunger flared hotter than before, but he set to work, fastening the chain holding the tiny shimmering ruby against her skin. The emerald green of her gown highlighted the alabaster perfection of her skin.

When he was done, he turned her. "Not tonight, *ma belle*?"

The sapphire blue of her eyes glinted in the light. "Come," she beckoned, and he followed, his gaze falling to the parcel wrapped in brown paper. "Open it," she demanded.

He took the edge of the string and pulled. It came away, and a purple wrapping of Indian silk lay beneath.

"That too," she whispered, her gaze burning him.

With careful touches, he unwound the material, and a book emerged. The cover of leather and Sanskrit script caught his attention. He opened the book, his breath catching.

"A pillow book?" He turned to look at her, wondering not for the first time at the amazing woman he'd married.

"You know what this is?" He heard the surprise in her voice.

He pulled her close, and his laugh rumbled against her belly. "Yes. I've seen one or two previously, though not as highly detailed as this one. Where did it come from?"

Isabelle ducked her head, and a rush of warmth settled deep inside him.

"Elspeth gave it to me. She received it as a wedding gift from an Indian princess. She thought we might find it...interesting."

He smiled. "You've seen one before?"

She blushed delightfully. "I have seen this one before. I mean..."

His grin grew wider. "Really? When?"

She turned away, and he placed the book down on the bed, finger slipping beneath her chin and turning her gaze back to him. "Isabelle?"

"Elspeth had it open in her cabin one day. I went down to find her parasol, and it was there."

"You looked." He spoke carefully, not wanting to surprise her. "I... Yes." The answer was little more than a whisper.

"Did it intrigue you?"

Her eyes widened, but she was no coward and faced him head-on.

He knew well-bred young women didn't talk of the marriage bed or pleasure, and he knew she'd learned that lesson from her aunt. "Yes."

"When we come home, we can look through it. Together."

Isabelle dropped her eyes. "But is that seemly?"

"Isabelle, in our chamber, whatever we do together is acceptable. So long as we are both comfortable and agree to it. If that means looking at a pillow book, then it is more than allowable. I would never do anything you weren't comfortable with. Remember last night?"

Her eyes glowed, as did her cheeks, a rosy color. "Yes."

"So, we can explore this when we come home." He dipped in, dropped a kiss on her lips, wanting more but knowing anything else would keep them home for the evening. "Now, come, wife. We have an engagement to attend."

Her arm wound around his, fingers in kidskin gloves resting on his jacket, and together they left the room.

At the bottom of the stairs, Mei waited with a long, white

rabbit-fur cape. "Mrs. Hargraves said it will snow tonight. She thought this might be better than a wrap." The girl pressed the heavy cloak into Isabelle's hands.

"Then I shall, of course, wear it."

He took the wrap and assisted his wife to put it on.

"Now, we shall away." He waved his arm and Mei scurried to open the door, and they stepped out.

Chapter Twelve

ISABELLE FLOATED in Langdon's arms as the final dance of the evening filled the air. The ball at Lady Mellington's had been well attended; the crush of bodies crammed into the room extreme and the air suffocating. In the end, they joined the stragglers heading out of the ballroom, thanking their hostess and waiting for Isabelle's cape and Langdon's outer jacket.

The air was sprinkled with flecks of white, and Isabelle reached out a gloved hand. "Snow? Mei said it might, but really? It snows in Shanghai? I would never have thought it could!"

He grinned at her delight. "I believe this happens from time to time, my dear." Their carriage rumbled up, and he ushered her into it. "Come."

She climbed in, shivering in the cold, then Langdon followed, and the carriage swayed as he settled beside her. The white rabbit of her cape stark against his coat. He tapped the roof with the walking stick, and they moved on. She nestled in his arms.

"You enjoyed yourself tonight, *ma belle.*"

Considering his words, Isabelle wondered how to explain

the joy she'd felt on the dance floor. After her mother had died, although her father had allowed dance classes, when she'd come of age, both she and Elspeth had been denied their Coming Out they'd expected and social events. Instead, they'd taken to assisting their father with the day-to-day running of the business.

In India she'd initially been too unwell, then later on, while she'd participated in the dancing, she'd not found a worthy partner. That was why early on in their courtship, she'd refused to dance.

"Yes, I did enjoy it."

They traveled in silence until suddenly, the carriage jerked to a halt. "Get out of the carriage!" a voice cracked through the night, and Langdon jolted in his seat.

"Stay here," he instructed her and dropped the window, peering outside.

He swore a vicious curse and turned to her. "It seems we're being held up. Slip your ring into your bodice quickly."

Isabelle stared at him then set about the task of removing her ring and necklace and sliding them between the mound of her breasts. She'd just finished when the door jerked open.

"Get out!" A masked man brandished a pistol, and Langdon assisted her down and pulled her close by the side of the road. "You!" He jerked the pistol at Isabelle. "Your jewelry!" She wrenched off her earrings, thankful they weren't the ones her mother had left her.

The man ripped them from her grasp. He then turned to Langdon, who'd pulled the pin from his ascot and the watch from his pocket.

The air turned frigid, with flakes of snow falling faster, and Isabelle shivered, tugging the rabbit fur close around her. The man stepped up, but Langdon came between them.

"Leave her be. She's given you what you demanded."

Eyes glittered behind the barrier of the handkerchief tied around the man's face. "I want her cape," he growled.

"She'll freeze," Langdon answered.

"Not my problem. Cape or bullet." The man spoke with a lilt, and Isabelle rushed to obey. The night air settled on her skin, chilling her instantly.

What more could happen?

The man leered then turned, cuffing Langdon, who fell to the ground. Isabelle cried out as the man retreated. As they left, she heard multiple voices talking, and the sound of horses' hooves clopping on the roadway echoed but soon died away.

"Help!" she cried, but no one came as iciness settled into her bones.

She knelt beside her husband, shaking his shoulder and hoping for assistance, while the snow fell. Tears leaked from her eyes as she called to Langdon.

"Wake up, Langdon. Please!" Terror streaked through her.

A sound, little more than a shuffle, caught her attention, and she looked up. Their driver, his face bloodied, came into sight, limping and holding his head in his hand. "Get into the carriage, Missus. I'll get your man in, and we'll head for the house."

Their coachman wasn't old, at least, but she knew he'd struggle. "If I help, we can get him inside quicker."

Langdon groaned as the two of them worked to raise him from the ground. "Isabelle?"

"I'm here, Langdon. Come, we need to get into the carriage." Her teeth chattered as the wind whipped around them. The horses were stomping the ground.

"Your cape," he whispered.

"We need to get inside." The cold which had settled inside her was dissipating now. Was it warming up?

She climbed in first, her fingers fumbling on the door, and Langdon followed with the driver pushing him from the rear. He settled in the seat, and in the light of the lantern, Isabelle could see a dribble of blood on the side of his face.

The driver slammed the door and quickly headed to his seat.

She heard him calling to the horses. They moved along, keeping a sensible pace in the worsening weather, the entire time Isabelle aware that the men who'd robbed them could be anywhere.

She didn't breathe fully until they entered the gates and reached the portico. She couldn't stop the shivering that set in, her entire body shuddering.

The driver ran up the steps, calling for assistance, and Fuchs, Mei, and even Mrs. Hargraves, along with a footman, came running.

They assisted Langdon then herself out of the conveyance and into the house. Mei ran to collect a warm wrap, Mrs. Hargraves her smelling salts and bandages, and Fuchs to retrieve hot water.

"I was frightened, Langdon," she whispered, her limbs trembling as warmth slowly re- entered her body. Now the tears were those of pain, as every nerve contracted with the return of heat to her extremities.

"I know," was all he said. His mouth was grim.

Mei rubbed at her arms, then wound the wrap around Isabelle's arms before attending to the fire. It pumped out heat, and Isabelle could barely form the words to still Mei's anxious movements.

Mrs. Hargraves bathed Langdon's cut and declared that he wouldn't need the physician. Isabelle didn't know if she agreed, but judging by the weather considered no one would likely come anyway, so she kept her silence.

Once they'd been attended to, she and Langdon rose, heading for their bedchambers. Mei unfastened Isabelle's gown and she dismissed the girl for the night, well aware of the hour. She slipped into a cambric nightgown, doubting Langdon would join her, and climbed into the large bed.

More tears threatened, but she refused to give in to them.

Since her marriage, she'd already survived two major mishaps. A third, and they may not be so lucky. She refused to give in, having finally made a connection that filled her with hope for the future.

The connecting door rattled, then opened, and Langdon walked through slowly, his face wan but very welcome.

"Langdon." She began to pull away from the bedcovers.

"No need," he muttered and made his way over to her, the dressing gown she'd seen the night before encasing him.

As he reached the bed, he pulled at the knot, and the firelight played over his naked skin. Her mouth dried as he climbed into the bed.

He held his arms out, and she burrowed in, unable to do other than give in to the fear and dread that had assailed her since the carriage had been stopped.

"I didn't think we'd survive," she hiccupped after the bout of crying passed.

He tugged her closer. "I don't know who or what is behind these things, but we'll find them, Isabelle."

She reared back. "You think they're connected?" Fury scoured her now. If that was the case, then she wanted to see them face justice.

"I can't see how they can't be. Two in one day is far too much a coincidence. Now come, sleep, and allow our bodies time to heal." He settled her down against his shoulder once more, and she couldn't help but clutch him close.

"Don't leave me," she muttered.

"I won't, *ma belle*. Now sleep. Rest, and we'll look at what we know in the morning." She hoped it would be that simple. It was only when the beat of his heart settled and she could hear the easy rhythm of his sleep that she relaxed enough to drift.

He woke. Alone. He turned, groggy, and reached for Isabelle. Her spot in the bed was cold, and for a moment his heart stuttered before he saw the indentation of her head on the pillow.

He sat up and there she was, at the small escritoire, writing in a book. "Isabelle?"

She turned. "I didn't want to wake you." She closed the tome, then pushed up, walking to the bed. "How do you feel?" She laid a gentle hand against his forehead.

"My head aches somewhat, but apart from that, I'm fine."

She settled on the side of the bed. "I have some tea here for you." She passed the cup, and he frowned, noting she was dressed in a warm woolen gown of blue.

"How long have you been awake?"

She bit her lip and looked away. "It's ten in the morning. I sent Mei and Fuchs away." He sighed. "We should rise." He attempted to, but she pushed hard against his chest. "The snowfall last night was deep. I doubt any business will take place today. Besides, it's Sunday."

"You wish me to stay here today?"

Isabelle nodded. "I would appreciate that. A quiet and restful day, then tomorrow, if you feel well, a short workday. I need to send a letter to Staindhouse. He can come to me in the short- term, but I will need to travel soon, Langdon. I must find new suppliers, and meet with those who already supply us. I can't rest. I have letters to write, instructions to give."

He sighed, aware she still had a business to attend to. He hoped they could solve the issues at hand well before that became a pressing eventuality though.

"Then, today, we will spend quietly. Recovering and attempting to work out how we can deal with these issues."

Langdon pushed the covers aside and rose. Fuchs had left the clothing for him in the dressing area of his bedroom, and though he protested, Isabelle followed through to assist him in dressing for the day.

The intimacy of the act wasn't lost on him.

Once attired, they headed downstairs, and they both ate a hearty breakfast.

The day passed slowly, Isabelle reading and sewing, though she disclaimed any real skill or interest in the latter pursuit. He read the paper, then opened a book his mother had sent him at yuletide. *L'Assommoir* was the continuation of a series he'd begun years earlier, but today it failed to grab his attention.

He retreated from the library in the early afternoon, catching Isabelle as she settled in with Mrs. Hargraves to discuss meals, and feeling at loose ends, he headed for the greenhouse, the place where he'd proposed to Isabelle.

The scent of the earth once more centered him, and he thought of home for the first time in months. Of his family. His mother, with her French accent and gesticulations. His father, with a bushy mustache, his pipe, and tweed. How he missed his sisters and their offspring and his brother. The lush, green fields of their main house. The horses he'd ridden and the friends he'd left behind. How would Isabelle fare so far from the coast and her beloved ships?

He and Isabelle were so different. He'd been raised in comfort with his loud family and doting parents. Always aware that one day the responsibility for leading the entire family would be his.

His mind flashed to the small estate in Suffolk where his mother had grown up with a distant relation. Though his mother had been born in France, her parents had emigrated when she was a young child, escaping the next wave of unrest that followed the dissolution of Charles X's monarchy and the July Revolution as it was now known. When the relation died, the property passed to his grandparents until their death the year his mother married his father. The property had passed as part of her inheritance to the family estate.

The tidy abode of Favermore Hall near Lowestoft would give them the freedom to continue their intimate education without the constant scrutiny of his family, yet close enough to visit his parents irregularly.

It was only two miles from Lowestoft, and while its port catered to the fishing industry, he was sure there was sufficient infrastructure should Isabelle wish to relocate Forster Shipping there.

He turned and headed for the house, his mind clear. Once this investigation was concluded, if she agreed, he'd request the house from his father for himself and his bride.

She was alone when he entered the parlor, dozing. "Isabelle?"

She roused, her eyes sleep-misted, her lips full, and it took everything he had to concentrate.

"Yes, Langdon?"

"I wanted to discuss returning to England with you." He took the seat beside her, watching as she jerked upward.

"You're not sending me back." Fire glinted in her eyes, and he smiled, well aware his woman was a fighter to the end.

"Not at all," he drawled. "But once my investigation is done, and you've completed your tasks, it will be time to return to England."

Isabelle subsided, waiting and listening, her eyes alight with interest. "Tell me what you're thinking."

"My mother is French. I'm not sure I ever told you that?" When Isabelle shook her head, he continued. "Her family emigrated after the later revolution in 1830. They lived with a distant uncle in Suffolk. The house where they lived is near Lowestoft, and when this distant uncle died, it ended up in my father's hands. It's currently empty. My mother disliked the house, saying her uncle was as cold as the house itself. Father had it updated, but as I said, she dislikes it, so they never visit.

Now, I would imagine you'd want to continue running Forster Shipping, so you need to be close to the sea. I can't promise we could relocate to your home, but there's a deep harbor in Lowestoft, suitable for your craft to dock. If there are no appropriate buildings for warehousing, we could construct what you need."

She gazed at him, her mouth dropping open. "You'd do that? For me?"

He gave a laugh, strangled with embarrassment. "I would, Isabelle. I won't ask you to give everything up."

She launched herself at him, laughing. "You're an exceptional husband already, Langdon. Thank you."

Monday morning dawned, and before Isabelle could leave the house, Langdon insisted the footman and Mei travel with her. "I'll have my man organize an armed escort for you today. For now, go straight to the wharf. Fuchs will stay with you and return at the same time. Send me a note once you've arrived safely."

"I will, but stay safe yourself."

He was still pale, but she forbore mentioning it, aware that his concern was solely for her. She wondered if all men were like that then shrugged the thought away. It was, after all, inconsequential. Isabelle rugged up in a woolen gown of dark blue, a heavy coat and gloves, and ventured into the cold.

Langdon would put in a half-day and meet her back at the house by mid-afternoon, and she planned to accomplish much in the next several hours. First, she wanted all the details of the crane disaster, then to check the losses they'd suffered.

The carriage moved through the banked snow, though by now it had turned a dirty, slushy brown. Not many traveled. "Too cold," Isabelle told herself, and while she could have put off today's excursion, that would put her plans severely behind.

They arrived at the warehouse, and she smiled, noting the puffing of the chimney. "Excellent. Staindhouse has the fire burning."

They entered the building, and she requested the complete list of losses, the manifest, and details of the information the captain had shared regarding the crane failure.

The morning passed slowly, with Mei offering tea, Staind-house hovering anxiously, and Fuchs waiting patiently.

"The list of china is where, Staindhouse?" He grimaced at her request, and her stomach dropped. "What?"

"They're all special pieces, Mrs. Deveraux. Made to order for the Duchess of Ainsley."

"Oh no! Did anything survive?"

His smile was thin. "The statuary, and some other pieces, so perhaps half the total number of items, and thankfully, they were the most expensive pieces."

"Get me a complete list. We'll have to arrange replacements forthwith."

Now she stood, pacing. These kinds of losses could hurt a shipping line, given the items would be late arriving at their location. She made a note in her book to ensure they were personally delivered with her compliments.

"And the report on the failure?"

Staindhouse blanched. "I have the information. The captain says there was a previous issue, but nothing that should compromise the hoist, otherwise he wouldn't have used it." He handed over the sheaf of papers.

She read them while her mind tossed over Langdon's fears that there was a concerted effort to damage Forster Shipping.

"Which vessels are due in the next three months?" She bit her lip and read through the list. The *Zephyr*, the *Lord Haver-sham*, and the *Penryn Coast* were due soonest, depending on the weather of course. Each swift and reliable. "And how many usually require passage on them?"

"Well, the captains don't like carrying passengers, so we do attempt to limit them to only three or four aboard a ship. We are, after all, a trading line. But we have an urgent request from Mrs. J. Elgin, a widow returning home. I had thought the next available berth might be suitable."

The clock in the corner chimed the hour of midday. She rose. "Send any further information to me, Staindhouse, and I will be in touch soon. I also would like the list of current suppliers, suggested traders, and so on." She turned to the door, accepting the coat Mei pressed on her. "Oh, and the report of the incident and the status with finding the man who assisted me."

"Very good, Mrs. Deveraux." Staindhouse bowed low as she reached for the door. Langdon should be home, and she might perhaps discuss these very few developments with him. It left her frustrated with how little information they'd so far managed to cobble together.

Once more, the trip was uneventful, and she arrived home, tugging off her gloves and entering the hall as Langdon emerged at the top of the steps, a smile stretching across his face.

*L*angdon was frustrated. Settling into his office at the municipal authority building, he summoned one of the investigators. Stubens was unavailable, and even though he'd been co- opted to assist with the opium situation, he couldn't yet find a link between it and the danger he was sure his wife faced. He perched on the edge of his seat, hands folded on the desktop.

A young man in his thirties entered. "Yes, sir?"

Langdon cleared his throat, pushing down firmly on the

memory of his fury and worry. He needed to ensure the information he shared was unemotional. There wasn't a lot he could tell the man, but the jewelry and cape would stand out on the underground market here in Shanghai. Whoever had perpetrated the holdup either didn't need the funds he might gain from turning over the stolen goods or didn't realize the value of what had been taken.

Langdon indicated to the inspector to take a seat.

"Two nights ago, after the ball at Lady Mellington's, my wife and I were returning home, when our carriage was stopped. I was assaulted, my wife's earrings and her fur cape stolen." He narrowed his gaze. "There were at least three men. Only one talked to us, and his voice was English, but I couldn't place his accent. The jewelry stolen was a pair of heart-shaped ruby earrings. The cape is white rabbit fur, fastened with a gold clasp at the neck."

The inspector frowned. "And your losses, sir?"

"A stick pin. Gold with a small ruby and diamonds. Round ruby stone surrounded by the diamond chips. Engraved on the back with the initials L.A.D." They didn't take his ring though, likely didn't realize he'd wear one, and his gloves covered that fact. "That's odd," he spoke aloud.

"What?" The man sat forward in his seat.

"They don't know me. Didn't realize I wear a ring with the family crest or I'm sure they would have demanded it." Langdon held out his hand to display the ring. "And they didn't take my wife's rings either, and even though they would have been hidden by gloves..."

"They didn't know you were wed?" the man suggested.

"Likely not. So, they're more than likely operating under remote instruction. Taking direction from someone else who wasn't there."

He gave a description of the height and eye color he'd noted during the attack of the man, informed him of the other two men who had remained at a distance, and the injuries he and the driver had sustained.

"We'll want to interview your driver."

"Yes, I expected you would. He'll be available to you on request. He's a private carriage driver but well-respected," Langdon offered.

By the end of the meeting, rage fired inside him.

"We'll find him, Major. Have no doubt." The inspector left his office, but now Langdon was unable to settle. It seemed that being within the municipal authority had somehow ground the investigation of the opium smuggling to a standstill. Wholly unacceptable.

His head ached, not that he'd admit that to Isabelle, and when the clock chimed, Langdon stood, thankful it was time to return home. He left the office and gave the direction of the house to his assistant before he left the building.

Chapter Thirteen

ISABELLE FRETTED.

When Langdon had walked through the door today, she'd noted the lines of strain about his mouth. Her memories returning to their wedding night, she'd scurried downstairs and given the order to Mrs. Hargraves that a cold collation would be acceptable for the evening. She'd also given orders for refreshments to be sent up to her bedroom, then she'd hurried back upstairs.

At five in the afternoon, she called Mei and Fuchs together. *A simple matter of my giving instructions.* Once they arrived in her boudoir, she closed the door.

"Fuchs, is my husband resting?"

He smiled. "No, madam. He's bathing."

She nodded, more than aware of how refreshing a deep soak could be. "Excellent. I wish you to set out comfortable clothes for him, then you are both excused for the evening."

He raised an eyebrow. "Madam?"

The heat of a blush rose on her cheeks. "You can have tonight off, Fuchs."

He bowed. "As you wish." Then he withdrew from the room.

"Mei, you too may have the evening to yourself. I'll dress if you'll undo my gown." The girl looked scandalized.

"You don't need me?"

"Only tonight," she hurried to explain to the girl. She'd come to like the girl and hoped that soon she'd be able to raise the suggestion of Mei coming with her back to England when she left.

"Yes, madam. Which gown do you want?"

Her mind spun, then settled. "The pale blue tea-gown will be fine." Fitted to be worn without a corset, it was cinched with a darker blue sash and loose. It fitted her plans accordingly. "Also set out the candles," she said, and even to herself, her voice sounded choked.

"Yes, miss." The girl moved around the room, her movements precise.

With the gown laid on the bed, Isabelle rose and turned, giving Mei access to her back so the variety of clips and buttons could be undone, then the girl released the strings of her corset.

"I'll help you into this," Mei said, and the gown was over Isabelle's head and sliding over her curves.

"Go now," she shushed Mei from the room, the gown Isabelle had removed in hand.

She'd barely completed preparing the candles when the connecting door opened, and her husband strode in.

"You've given Fuchs and Mei the night off?"

She stepped closer. "Yes. Mrs. Hargraves and the rest of the staff too." Inside, her belly jittered with nerves, but Isabelle pushed them down, covering her fears with bravado.

He cocked his head to one side, his gaze questioning.

"I thought perhaps we could consider the gift from Elspeth," she whispered, and his gaze grew smoky.

"Madam wife, you engage me evermore daily."

The knot of anxiety that had lodged in her belly unwound

a little. "A cold collation is being laid in the dining room. I thought maybe we could——"

He'd crossed the room while she'd chattered, his arms winding around her. "Later," he murmured and kissed her. Deep and drugging. Her vision narrowed, and she closed her eyes, losing herself into the sensations he fanned within her.

His hand slid down her back and cupped her bottom, lifting her into his embrace.

Isabelle wanted to wind her legs around his waist, but the gown hampered her. "Darn," she growled.

He smiled, and it stole her breath. "Maybe we should eat."

The lump lodged in her throat threatened to choke her.

Langdon's grip eased, and she slid, gown slithering against his robe. The silk of her covering sliding against her already aroused body, and she groaned, biting her lip.

"Come," he murmured, and she shivered before taking the hand Langdon extended. His fingers wound around hers, and she followed him to the door.

Her gaze flew to the door, and he smiled widely.

"Come," he beckoned, and she scurried down the staircase, unimaginably embarrassed at being about in the house in just the sheer gown. His robe, loosely tied, flapped as he walked, and she had to swallow deeply, aware that he wore nothing else.

On the dining table lay a spread of cheeses, meats, and fruits, and Langdon settled into a seat, piling his plate high with the choices before him. A carafe of wine and two glasses shone under the chandelier as she settled beside him, picking from the array of choices. Satisfied that she'd chosen what she wanted, Isabelle nibbled on some cheese while Langdon poured the ruby wine into the crystal goblet and passed it to her.

The crackle of the fire was warming, and she settled back, still highly aware but now slightly less concerned that someone would enter the room.

"You know, in London, I heard of these clubs where they use a woman as the serving dish," Langdon intoned, and Isabelle choked on the cheese she'd just bitten.

"What?" She turned to him, scandalized. "You are surely jesting?"

His visage was full of humor. "Not at all, my dear. The women are naked, spread out on the table, and they become the dish. Hellfire clubs they're called."

Isabelle wasn't sure if she was more scandalized or intrigued by the concept, but she didn't share her dilemma with her husband. What would he think of her if she did?

She bent her head and ate a little more, trying vainly to refocus her attention. *Bite. Chew. Swallow.*

"Isabelle?" He spoke softly, and she jumped.

"Langdon?"

"Is something amiss?" His brows furrowed, and she blushed.

"No."

"No?" He leaned over, just a bit, but it gave the impression of him concentrating harder on her.

Isabelle gulped. "No... I mean, I don't know."

His fork clattered onto the plate. "What are you having trouble with?"

Her hand flew to her mouth. "I..." She blushed, the heat radiating from her. "Women on the table." The words emerged sounding swollen and forced.

"Ahhh..." He settled back in his seat. "Hellfire clubs. Not really my kind of establishment. But were it you before me..." His mouth widened in a smile. His eyes flashed. "I could see you, miles of milky skin and strawberries, raspberries, and every luscious sweetness ready for me to partake. I'd feed directly from your skin, my tongue flicking against your breasts. Cream dribbled over your thighs..."

She blinked, the words arousing and tantalizing. Her body began the slow melt, and a throb started in her loins.

He stood and moved around beside her, reached over and slid a fingertip over one exposed collarbone.

"All for me. My pleasure and your pleasure. I wouldn't miss a single flavor, Isabelle. Every inch of your body."

His words tugged at some invisible cord within her, tweaking every erogenous zone so the hunger she'd tried hard to bank wanted to explode into life. The touch of his finger slowly rubbing against her skin was drugging. Her eyelids drooped.

"Stand up, Isabelle," he whispered, and she did, the chair behind her seeming to move of its own volition.

Without conscious thought, Isabelle reached beneath the lapels of his dressing gown, seeking the skin he hid from her gaze.

Their gazes met, and she read heat and hunger in his eyes. His fingers moved; she felt them sliding over the gown, but when it slid open, she gasped, then realized her own had found the cord fastening of his, her fingers worrying the knot.

"Unfasten it, Isabelle," he murmured, and she did, so it too gaped and displayed him for her to feast her gaze upon.

He slipped the gown from her shoulders, and it slid, pooling to the floor, and while she watched, he did the same with his own.

She shivered as the sensuality of the moment impressed on her. Anyone might come in and find them naked. Yet there was a confidence clothing Langdon far more effectively than any scrap of cloth might.

He pulled her close, so their bodies touched, and kissed her gently before tugging away. "We should finish our meal," he said.

"But—"

For a moment, shock coursed as he strode back to his seat, the knowledge of their bare bodies urging her to do the same. "Finish your meal, Isabelle, before I decide to gorge upon you."

"But—"

"We're alone, Isabelle. You gave the staff the night off. And since I am with the most delightful woman who just happens to be my wife, I intend to enjoy you and your company. So, let's eat, then we can retire."

It didn't settle the wild hammering of her pulse, but Isabelle couldn't argue with the logic. They were alone, or at least she hoped, so she turned her attention to the food. It was erotic, the nakedness. Every time she reached, her breast would scrape against the wooden tabletop, and she sucked in more than one gasp of awareness. When they'd done, he topped up their glasses.

They rose, and she gathered up the clothing they'd scattered. He gave her a look of understanding, and with glasses and clothes in hand, they made their way up the staircase toward their chambers.

Langdon opened the door, and Isabelle followed him within.

She dropped the clothing on the chaise as he slid the glasses onto the large stand beside the bed.

"Come." He climbed onto the bed and patted the spot at his side.

Inhaling deeply, Isabelle dropped to her knees at the foot of the bed, opened the trunk there, and removed the satin-wrapped tome, then she stood and made her way to the side of the bed.

Before she climbed on, she reached for the covers, but Langdon stilled her. "No. Join me."

She climbed onto the bedcovers and waited as he took the heavy parcel from her grasp.

"A pillow book," he murmured, sliding the heavy silk from the book. "Centuries ago, they were painted by artists. Given to those newly married, and the richer the title decorations, the more important the owner. Sexuality was far more open."

"How do you know all this?" Even to herself, her voice sounded breathy and insubstantial.

"I've been intrigued by them for a long time, Isabelle."

He opened the book, his gaze taking in the jeweled tones. He turned the page, his gaze sharpening on the image depicted. The ruby red and emerald green of the print bright of the page, adding depths to the joy on the couple's faces, where they lay on a divan, the woman's breasts exposed and the man's hands cupping her flesh—the act both carnal and yet incredibly intimate.

"He worships her, fondles her, and yet all the while he supports her, so she's able to give herself fully to the pleasure."

Isabelle gulped as he spoke. Every word was dragging her deeper into the web of desire. He turned the page again and again until he reached one etched in ruby and onyx. "This time, the heat of their passion. See how their bodies are joined, Isabelle. They both assume an equal status in the act of loving."

Her body ached for more as she gazed upon Langdon's face, alive with interest. "But isn't the..." She coughed a little, unsure how to proceed. "I mean, it's supposed to be a duty."

He laughed, put the book aside, and turned to her fully, cupping her cheeks in his hands. "Does this feel like a duty to you?"

The question didn't require thought. "No," she answered.

"Excellent. Then let me tell you, as you become more used to loving, we can find an equal footing. You give, and I give equally so that the pleasure is always about both of us. The same as we can introduce different aspects to lovemaking. Oils and candles help to enhance the mood." His hand moved in slow, methodical circles, and she arched beneath his ministrations.

"Langdon? I want you to love me." She slid down the pillows.

The grin on his face became wide. "Oh, I intend to. Let

me think..." He assumed a position of concentration, his eyes alight with mischief as he took in her nakedness arrayed for him. "I want to suck your nipples, *ma belle*. They're pretty and pert, strawberry-tipped mounds that beg for my touch."

She gave a squeak, and he leaned forward, opening his mouth over the distended nub. His tongue curled, and she bowed up, the curl of heat ribboning through her body from groin to breast and back again.

His hand slid down over her belly and cupped her mound, fingertips massaging the sensitive flesh as she slid her legs apart, wordlessly requesting still more.

"Lang... Langdon!" Her moans filled the air like the scent of musk rose winding around them.

His mouth moved again, this time to her ribs, and she breathed in, eyes blind from pleasure as one finger slid between swollen flesh to find the nubbin of pleasure and pressing on it.

Isabelle dragged her legs together as her body spiraled, lost in a web of sensuality.

His laugh was tight. "Not yet, *ma belle*. Your turn. Touch me."

The words broke through the fog. "Touch you?" Her eyes opened, she blinked once then again. "How?"

"Any way you like. Tell me what you'd like to do."

The thud of her heart was slow, and she allowed her gaze to roam over his body. Dips and planes that she so desperately wanted to touch and learn. Biting her lip, Isabelle reached out and touched the length of his engorged penis. "I want to know if you're hard or soft," she whispered. Fear and excitement warred equally within her.

"Then find out, Isabelle." His chest moved, and she noted the fine sheen of sweat coating his skin.

With a shaking fingertip, she slid it over the head, then pulled away when his cock jerked. "Did I hurt you?"

Langdon curled his hand around hers, pulling it back over

his flesh. "God, no, *ma belle*. You touch me carefully. I'm just sensitive with want. For you." His voice had turned gravelly, and she felt the shocking explosions of awareness with every word.

She squeezed a little, and he hissed, hand still over hers, and she felt the tremor of him.

"More," he demanded, and she did, this time her hand sliding up and down the long shaft, and Langdon groaned. "That feels so good," he crooned.

Awe suffused her. That she could do this to him made her feel powerful.

Then he moved, brushing her hand away. "Too much and I won't last, *ma belle*."

Now he kissed her lips, mouth ravaging and demanding as he pulled her closer. Nipples scraped across his chest as he hauled her closer, then over him. He was draping her sensually like a sheet over his abdomen.

Her legs widened and slid down beside his so she bracketed him. She felt the tip of his cock nudged at the apex of her thighs and looked down. "Langdon?" Surprise and excitement engulfed her. Could she? How was this even possible?

His drugged gaze met hers, and the excitement roared deep inside at the primal hunger that she saw on his face. "Yes, Isabelle."

He clasped her hips with hard fingers. Pulled her closer, so his cock nestled against the pearl, then shifted until he slid deep and sure within her body.

"Oh God," she cried as the touch fired off rocket explosions inside her body. The tension was winding her higher and higher. She flung back her head. "Langdon," she moaned as he slid deep within then moved. The act natural and gentle, yet it claimed every inch of her.

Heart. Body. Soul.

"Langdon," she crooned as they undulated to an unheard erotic rhythm.

Passion radiated throughout her. He nipped at her shoulder, kissed her neck, and demanded more wordlessly. She met him equally, giving the same pleasure and adulation he heaped upon her.

The fiery dance sped faster. Each thrust satisfying and harder. Each slide met with a rasping breath. Her heart beat a rapid tattoo.

The precipice loomed, a shining second of clarity before the wild explosion of an orgasm. She gave in to the all-encompassing rapture, body straining for every last ounce of ecstasy. Somewhere in the deep recesses of her mind, she felt him jerk then released the last strands of conscious thought.

Langdon held her, body to body, though she now slumped, soaked from the exertions.

Spent from the power of their lovemaking.

"Isa-belle," he muttered, the cadence of his voice lulling her even as her eyes closed and she slept.

Chapter Fourteen

IN THE EARLY hours of the morning, Langdon woke. Isabelle remained cuddled by his side, her hair framing her face, relaxed in sleep.

He rubbed at his bleary eyes then slipped from the bed. He gathered up the pillow book, hunted for the heavy silk saree she'd kept it wrapped in, and made his way to the end of the bed and the old trunk which sat there.

"Such a small thing," he murmured, his gaze returning to the bed where his wife slept.

He covered the book and slid it into the wooden trunk and returned to the bed. Carefully easing the covers from under her, he moved in beside her cool body. With the covers now warming them, he tugged her close.

"What..." she husked.

"Just pulling the covers up, *ma belle*."

She smiled, sleepy and heavy, and something in his chest lurched. He wasn't yet ready to name the emotion, but it was growing and taking on a life of its own. If only he could keep her safe. His gaze wandered to the window. Beyond the house, unless his men or himself were with her, he couldn't guarantee her safety. That knowledge rode him hard.

"Langdon?" Her hand cupped his cheek.

He gave her his full attention. "What, *ma belle?*"

"Thank you." Her eyes fluttered closed.

He wanted to ask her what for. Was it for the loving they'd shared? Was it because he'd started teaching her about loving and ways of eastern sexuality? Was it something different? He didn't know if he was ready to find out.

Instead, Langdon settled down, drawing her into his arms, and closed his eyes, determined to sleep.

Chapter Fifteen

ISABELLE COULDN'T CONTROL the smile that filled her face. Last night had been an adventure into a world of sensuality she could never have guessed existed. Langdon had loved her thoroughly and allowed her to explore and learn. To be an equal partner in their relationship, and it occurred to her that perhaps not too many women were given the freedom to express themselves the way she had.

The carriage rolled to a halt outside the warehouse, and she climbed down, only dimly aware of Mei, who traveled with her. She'd also accepted the man who moved behind them, on horseback, as a guard. She knew Langdon was concerned, though why still didn't make much sense. How could his investigations impact on her?

She spied the door of the building, shocked to see that it was cracked open but there was no sign of Staindhouse.

"Mr. Staindhouse?" she called and pushed the door open.

A curse echoed behind her, and the guard, Martin, swung down from his horse. "Wait, madam. Let me check." He brushed past her and entered the room.

Isabelle hovered by the door, her fingers clenched as a wave of concern rose.

The man returned, having checked the building quickly. "No one here. But there is something that concerns me. I need to send someone for Mr. Stubens, and the major will want to be notified too."

She glanced over her shoulder as the driver crowded in behind her. "I can go to the major. He can send for Stubens himself," he offered. "But I'll take the horse. It'll be quicker, and you keep the carriage in case you need to leave."

Martin nodded his agreement. "Yes. Be back here as quickly as you can." He then ushered Isabelle and Mei into the room and latched the door, no doubt assuming the driver would unhitch the horse or at least arrange it to be tethered while he rode back to Langdon's office.

"Martin, did you find something?" Isabelle enquired, after considering the man who waited in the small warehouse office.

"Yeah. But we should wait for your husband."

If nothing else raised her ire, it was being treated like some useless female. But perhaps she was misreading the situation, she considered. "What have you found?"

His face screwed up. "Being a lady, I don't think..."

Now Isabelle did take umbrage. "I may be a lady, but this is my shipping line, Martin. I make the decisions, and I will decide what I need to know or don't." Stepping up to the man, she noted with satisfaction that he blinked. Perhaps he'd think twice before treating another woman like a lesser being.

"Of course, Mrs. Deveraux. I found a pot with a brown substance. I think it may be opium resin."

She took a step back. Opium resin? "Show me," she demanded, her voice sounding strangled.

He lurched into the warehouse, and she followed him. In the center, there was a large ginger pot. Smashed. Around it oozed the resin, mixed with what appeared to be tobacco. She knew what that was, but crouched down anyway, desperate to assure herself it couldn't be so. She had seen it once before when her father had shown both herself and Elspeth.

The cold lump in the pit of her belly told her it was as she dreaded. "That's opium."

Martin grunted, watching her intently.

She whirled. "No one is to enter this area until I give the order. My husband will wish to see this. I'll also need to find Staindhouse and see what he knows." She turned a wide circle, her gaze taking in the stacks, and noted a pile, just slightly disordered, to the rear.

"Mrs. Deveraux?"

"There's something wrong. Staindhouse is very exact with the placement of cargo. He and I were working on cleaning it up." He'd been doing so well since she'd arrived. It felt wrong.

The slow thud of her heart matched the sudden fear in her belly. She advanced toward the stack.

"Did you come to the back?" she asked Martin.

"No, Mrs. Deveraux. I just checked to see..."

She reached the stack, fingers curling into the palm of her hands, and peered over. She nearly lost her breakfast when, peering beyond, she spied a pair of feet.

"Oh Lord." Isabelle sped up, hurried around the boxes, and stopped, eyes settling on the sightless gaze and puddle of blood. "Staindhouse."

A commotion caught her attention, and she turned, her husband there already, his gaze wild. "Isabelle."

She choked on a sob. "It's Staindhouse. Dead. There's opium in the pot on the floor. What's happening, Langdon?" The final words released on a wail, and Langdon folded her in his arms.

Gripping tightly to the cloth of his jacket, she breathed in the scent of this man and accepted the support he wordlessly offered.

They stood there, wound around each other for long moments before she stepped back. "We need to send for the constables." Her voice sounded strained, as if she'd been screaming.

"I've already done that. Come now, into the office, and we'll have Mei prepare a cup of tea." He moved her away from the body. The sight of the man, the pool of scarlet liquid had already seared itself into her mind. "There's more to this than meets the eye, Isabelle," he stated, and she wanted to pull away and ask why. But with Martin in attendance, she refused to query his soft comment. Martin had already questioned her authority, and she wouldn't put Langdon in the same situation.

Langdon settled her in a seat and sent Mei to arrange tea.

"Staindhouse would have been here by himself?" he queried

"Yes. He would come into the office, prepare the day's tasks, accept deliveries, and check the items before adding the information to the manifest. He had informed me that today he'd be meeting with new suppliers of ceramics. Such as the ginger jar."

Her belly shifted as she understood it was likely that the people Staindhouse was planning on meeting with could have also been his attackers. She shied away from calling them murderers, but the knowledge was there, in her brain.

Langdon paced the room, and Isabelle watched as he considered her answer. "And you don't know the identity of these suppliers he was planning to meet?"

Isabelle shook her head. "No. But that wasn't uncommon. Usually, the man of business conducts these negotiations once we've specified the number and types of products we are seeking. Sometimes we already have an existing relationship. Sometimes the new supplier comes to us through word of mouth."

"And this one?"

She frowned. "Staindhouse said they'd contacted him. He'd never had dealings with them before, but they'd appeared legitimate from the investigations he'd carried out. We only deal with reputable companies, Langdon." Even as she added the qualifier, it left her wondering who Staindhouse had spoken with to gain the assurances. She bit her lip. "I should have—"

His gaze blazed. "No. If you'd been here..." Langdon blanched. "No, Isabelle. I can't lose you."

Something in the tone of his voice calmed the wild seesawing of her emotions. He cared enough that losing her would hurt. As far as emotional declarations went, it was sufficient for now.

Isabelle stood as the door opened and in trotted three men. An older one who Langdon introduced as 'Stubens' and two younger men. They crowded into the small office, and Mei shrank back to the corner. One looked at Mei, and his gaze narrowed. "A Chinese girl?"

Once more, Isabelle's ire rose. "My maid," she answered and stared the young man down. He blushed and concentrated on his notepad.

Both Langdon and Isabelle settled into seats, as did Stubens before the investigator began questioning Langdon. Then he turned to Isabelle. "Mrs. Deveraux, you found the body?"

"Yes. In the warehouse. We arrived and there was no one here, though the door was open a little."

"You didn't see anyone when you arrived?"

"No. But when we realized the door was open, Martin here checked inside quickly. Seeing no one, he let Mei and myself in. I sent the driver for the major and entered the warehouse to investigate. That's when the jar was discovered and the opium resin."

Stubens's eye quirked. "You knew what it was?"

On a sigh, Isabelle folded her hands together. She was used to men questioning her knowledge of the man's world, but it did exhaust her. "Yes. My father ran Forster Shipping for many years. As my sister and I started to take more active roles, he was insistent we should know what to be aware of. Opium is one of the trades we refuse to participate in, and my father felt we should know what the resin looked like and how it was used so we could be aware."

The man stared at her, then nodded. "Oh. Yes, of course. So, what happened then?"

She shuddered. "After I'd seen the jar, I noted a stack of cases were out of order. Staindhouse was particular about the way things were stacked. He kept a tidy warehouse, with each item categorized and stored in order. I went to investigate and found him there."

The burn of nausea threatened again, but she pushed it down. She would not embarrass either herself or Langdon by displaying weakness, she told herself firmly.

Stubens asked some other questions then rose to confer with his men before excusing himself. He wandered into the warehouse, and as the younger men followed, Isabelle deflated. Exhausted and horrified by what she'd seen.

"Go home," urged Langdon. "I'll follow as quickly as I can."

She rose to argue that she should remain, but Stubens re-entered the warehouse so she sank back down to the seat she'd vacated. "Mrs. Deveraux, you should go home. You too, Major. My men and I will complete our investigation here, then visit Mr. Staindhouse's wife and inform her of his death. We'll post a man here, and when your workers arrive, we'll—"

Now she bolted upright again. "They're not here!" Isabelle felt foolish, but where were the men who assisted on the docks?

Stubens gazed at her as if she'd run mad.

Isabelle centered herself. "We usually have at least one man in attendance when there is no vessel due in port. They would carry out any heavy lifting tasks. But he's not here." She rose and went to Staindhouse's desk. Flitting through the piles, she found the worker's details and handed them to Stubens. "He comes in daily and has done so for the last three years according to Staindhouse, except Sunday and Monday. Today is Tuesday. So why isn't he here?"

Langdon took her hand. "Let Stubens check, and he'll report back with his findings, won't you?"

Stubens nodded. "Yes, Major."

It felt wrong to Isabelle to walk away, but her nerves were shredded, and the overlarge knot in her chest just appeared to keep growing. "Of course," she agreed.

Mei draped Isabelle's coat over her shoulders, and she allowed Langdon to walk her to the carriage and hand her in. Mei followed, and they waited while Langdon conferred quickly with Stubens then clambered in after them both.

"Home," he ordered, and the carriage turned a wide arc, and they headed from the wharf.

The whole way home, Langdon hashed over what they knew. The one overwhelming aspect was Staindhouse, Isabelle's man of business in Shanghai, was dead. Murdered in the warehouse not too long before she arrived, given the puddle of blood hadn't yet congealed. She'd found the body, and somehow opium was involved. He couldn't avoid the knowledge that she'd missed the killer by minutes, and that chilled him to the core.

Isabelle kept up the appearance of being in control, but he could see the toll it took, the way her eyes flicked from side to side, and the occasional shudder. Convention dictated that in front of her maid, he couldn't take her in his arms and offer comfort, and he chafed at that restriction.

When they arrived home, Langdon urged Isabelle upstairs to change into something more comfortable, and while that occurred, he headed to his office to write down what little facts they currently knew.

The investigations that had already taken place showed Forster Shipping did not carry opium, nor were they participating in the ferrying of intelligence against the crown. But somehow, Forster Shipping, and ergo, Isabelle, was involved and endangered.

"If only the answers could be divined on so little evidence," he muttered.

One link was all they needed—some speck of information that would offer clarity and allow them to find the perpetrator.

The door opened, and Isabelle entered the library then closed the door behind her with a gentle click.

"I haven't come at a bad time, have I?"

"No, Isabelle. I'm just trying to piece together the bits we do know. But this is like a puzzle, and we're missing the parts that will give us the answer." He stalked, frustrated and concerned, toward Isabelle then took her in his arms. "But you never choose a bad time. I will always be available to you."

"Thank you..." She stopped, her voice husky, then she bit her lip.

He crowded close, aware she needed to release the pressure that hammered inside her. "It's okay, Isabelle."

"But..." She shook her head, the dam walls breaking as she gave in, sobs wracking her body, and he held her.

He wished he could absorb her fears and loss. But he couldn't, so knowing that, he chose the next best action—holding her tight. Letting her release the pent-up emotions that he knew battered her.

The sound of her sobs and the way her body jerked scoured him. She cared deeply.

She wanted nothing more than to run her shipping line and learn about pleasure.

She was a kind woman.

A giving wife, and damn it, he loved her.

The acceptance of his emotional involvement stole his breath, and for a moment, he was sure it couldn't be, yet his more logical brain reminded him to trust himself and his emotions. "Thank you," she whispered and tugged away. His body wanted to hold tight, but he understood her need for distance, so she could stand on her own two feet, so to speak.

Isabelle wiped her face with a dainty handkerchief, and he waited until she'd quieted. "Sit down, Isabelle."

She acceded to his request, sinking into the seat opposite the desk.

A knock echoed on the door, and when permitted to enter, the door opened and in slid Mei. "I may speak with you?"

He nodded, and she stepped in, closed the door.

"I know about the opium," the girl whispered, and his gut lurched.

"What do you know?" He kept his voice low because the girl assumed the attitude of fear, in the way she hunched over and wound her arms around her small body.

Mei looked away, at Isabelle, then back. "The trade is with the white men. They came to China and brought opium from India. My... My father is one of them." Her voice wobbled on the last sentence, and Langdon fought the urge to close his eyes.

"How do you know this?"

Her head drooped, and Langdon waited.

Minutes passed, and Isabelle leaned toward the girl, touched her hand. "Mei?"

"He sells to Chinese men. They smoke it with tobacco, but he uses the girls he slaves for prostitution to distribute."

Langdon sighed. "Do you..."

"No!" The girl backed away, and the growing horror in Langdon's mind subsided a little. "I work. My father takes my money, but I not do this thing. These girls? They are stolen from their families. He sells their bodies for money and opium then sells to others. He's a bad man, Major. Very bad." Mei's voice broke, and Isabelle rose and pulled her close.

"It's okay, Mei. I won't let him hurt you." She gazed over Mei's head to Langdon.

As much as he wanted to promise that, he couldn't. The girl was young, and her father had rights—God, how he hated even acknowledging that right now.

"I will pass the information onto Stubens, but for now, Mei, you should stay here with my wife. I'll do everything I can."

The girl lifted her head, and on her young face, there was an anguished acceptance. "I know, when you leave, I will have to return home."

Isabelle made a strangled noise. "No, Mei. When we go, I want you to come with us. As my maid."

Mei squinted. "He must give permission. He won't allow this."

"Then we'll make him," countered Isabelle.

Langdon wanted to tell Isabelle that she was out of her depth. She didn't understand this pseudo-Chinese culture she was pitting herself against. Then he realized that Mei's father was English. Perhaps there was something that could be done?

"You can't—"

"Wait," he said at the same time as Mei. "There are ways. Leave this with us, Mei. We'll find a way to release you from your father."

Isabelle frowned. "What about your mother?"

Mei sighed. "She's dead."

The wooden way she spoke pierced him, but right now, it also meant one less complication to deal with. "We'll find a way, Mei. Now, prepare Mrs. Deveraux's clothes for dinner. We are to dine at Mrs. Althorp's tonight."

The girl left them, and Isabelle scoured his face. "Can we do something?" He smiled thinly. "There's always a way when money is involved."

*I*sabelle searched through the ledger on the desk, scanning for details of the new supplier as Langdon had requested.

Staindhouse had kept immaculate records of everything coming in and out. She wondered, not for the first time, how she'd replace him. The notification to Mrs. Staindhouse had been fraught, according to Stubens. He'd arrived on their stoop shortly after Mei had left the library.

Isabelle had determined she should pay a call on the widow, find a way to financially assist the woman if she could, and perhaps also check to see if there were any records in his home. Not that she'd told Langdon all of her plans. Only that she'd pay a condolence visit. He'd been unhappy but agreed.

So, now she waited for the carriage to arrive. Mei would remain home this time under Mrs. Hargraves's watch while she traveled with Martin as her guard and escort.

The rap on the door had her raising her head. "Yes?" she inquired of Mrs. Hargraves.

"Your carriage is here." The woman gazed at her, and Isabelle could read the unspoken concern in Mrs. Hargraves's gaze.

"I shouldn't be long. Have Mei prepare my silver gown for tonight, and on my return, I am due to meet with the dressmaker." The longer she remained in Shanghai, the stronger she'd become, but also the more fulsome her figure, and the gowns she'd had made needed further alterations. Besides, she wanted to order some more items, specially made to her specifications.

The thought of the special order she planned saw her through the quick trip to Staindhouse's lodging. When she arrived, it was to a small, slightly seedy area. Here there were alehouses, and she could see the remains of the old Woosung Road rail system. Martin informed her that it had only been pulled up within the last few years and shipped away after the locals had taken control of it.

Alighting from the carriage, she glanced around, hyper-aware of Martin's presence for protection. When she reached the door, there was the cry of a child echoing from within.

"Please wait out here, Martin," she said, and the man gazed at her, clearly unhappy. "But—"

"This is a condolence visit. I'm sure I'll be safe enough inside."

She knocked and waited, then the door opened and a young woman, barely two-and- twenty, if she didn't miss her mark, opened it. "Hello?" Her voice was querulous, eyes red and teary.

"I'm seeking Mrs. Staindhouse," Isabelle said.

The woman wiped her hands on her apron. "That would be me."

Shock and surprise filled Isabelle. "Your husband was—"

"Matthias Staindhouse." The young woman peered at her. "You'd have to be Mrs. Deveraux. Matthias, God bless his soul, told me you'd recently wed. Please come in."

Isabelle followed the woman inside and sat when invited.

Mrs. Staindhouse disappeared and returned with an infant. "Young Matthias here won't get to know his father," she whispered, her bottom lip quivering.

That stung Isabelle greatly. "I'm here first to pay my respects, but also because I wish to assist. I was unaware Matthias had a young family, and it seems to me, you'll be needing support."

The woman shot up out of her chair, her face red. "I want no charity."

Isabelle held out a hand. "That's not my intention. You have a child. A young child. Clearly, you have responsibilities here in the home, and I wish only to help you to raise your child."

Mrs. Staindhouse shook her head, wisps of brown hair

flying. "There's been enough talk of me over the years. My Matthias was a good man. He stood by me when my parents died, took me in, and raised me. When tongues started wagging, he wed me. Cared for me and eventually loved me. He gave me my little Matthias here. I won't let anyone talk about him like Shanghailanders do."

Isabelle frowned, spent a moment deep in thought. "Do you wish to stay here? In Shanghai?"

"No. But I don't know else."

"I have a sister. She is expecting her first child and will need a nanny. She wrote telling me she hasn't yet found one. I could send you there. Settle funds on you in case it doesn't work. You could raise your child well in your home country."

Mrs. Staindhouse frowned. "Why would you do that?" she whispered.

"Because your husband was a good and loyal employee. He cared about Forster Shipping, and we care for our employees. I can even arrange a cottage for you, your passage if you will let me."

Financially, the promises weren't large, but if the young woman had been subject to wagging tongues, perhaps a change of location and a fresh start for her and her child might be the assist she needed to get back on her feet.

"I'll think on it," she finally answered, and Isabelle knew she'd have to be grateful for that at this time.

"All right then. I'm also wondering if your husband kept any records at home. Who he was meeting with, his contacts, or new suppliers?"

The young woman's brow furrowed. "He did meet with a new supplier about two weeks ago. They gave him a pot and told him it was his to keep."

Isabelle leaned forward. "May I see it?"

Mrs. Staindhouse disappeared for a moment and returned with an ornate blue and white vase. "This. He said his new supplier had many more such pieces and we'd be able to add them to the shipments going out soon. He was that excited, Mrs. Deveraux. Told me Mr. Tang assured him the supply would be ongoing should he be happy with the items."

Isabelle took the vase offered and ran a calculating eye over it. "Nice and light. Good quality ceramic work. Tell me, how did he meet Mr. Tang?"

"Mr. Hooper at the alehouse introduced them. Said Mr. Tang was from a good family, and he knew them well. Personally, I wouldn't trust Hooper. Not with his business in girls."

"Hooper isn't a good man?"

"Matthias, bless him, always found the best in people. He said Hooper had a difficult time raising his daughter, but she was run wild, and he had to cut her off. Said how Hooper would have helped her more, but I knew her. She was a good girl and tried to look after the women he kept. Matthias though, he refused to accept that Hooper kept the girls chained up, like cattle."

Isabelle frowned. Business with girls? Chained up? Maybe she should check with Mei before she went any further.

"Thank you for your time, Mrs. Staindhouse. On behalf of Forster Shipping and my family, please accept our condolences on your loss. Consider the offer, as we make it in good faith." She rose, shook out her skirts, and extended a hand. The woman looked at it, and with great trepidation, she shook it.

"Thank you, Mrs. Deveraux. I will think about your offer. Matthias told me where you were staying, and once I make a decision, I'll send word."

Isabelle left the house, her mind reeling. No written information, but a name or two to follow up. She'd take that as a success.

*L*angdon stalked the length of the library, waiting for Isabelle to return. That she'd disappeared like this, at a time when he knew how much danger there was, infuriated him. "She has no idea of the chances she's taking," he groused, while every sound left him stilling in the hopes it might be Isabelle returning home.

The door handle to the library turned, and he whirled. When his gaze settled on hers, he released a pent-up breath.

"Langdon. Is all well?" she inquired, and he harnessed the anger that curled deep in his gut.

"No, Isabelle. All is not well. Why did you leave the house without me? I believe I made the situation and the danger clear to you."

Isabelle stilled. "I simply wished to see Mrs. Staindhouse. To ascertain if she required assistance and to offer my condolences. It's what I would do, no matter the situation. I did inform you of that."

Her lack of understanding staggered Langdon, who'd imagined everything from her being held up and sold into slavery—which he knew well enough did indeed happen in these civilized times—through to her death in a ditch.

"You have no idea of the worry I've experienced since receiving the intelligence you'd left the house. Isabelle, whoever is behind these atrocities is—"

"But I have a name. Well, actually two, for you, Langdon." She stepped closer, her eyes shining. "Mrs. Staindhouse told me her husband met with two people."

The words stopped him, and it took a moment to overcome his shock. "Names? You endangered yourself for two names?" he roared.

She stepped back. "Yes. No. Well, I was assisting you, as any good wife would do." God help her, he thought, unable to miss the hurt flashing through her eyes.

"I don't care for you to be dead, Isabelle. A man doesn't

easily accept that the woman he loves puts herself into danger in order to assist him."

Isabelle's mouth dropped open. "Love?"

He cursed himself in silence. He'd not meant to share his feelings like this. Instead, he'd planned to tell her quietly, in her boudoir. To romance her and whisper it into her ear, sure she'd shiver as he spoke. For now, though, he pushed on, letting his fright take over.

"For heaven's sake, Isabelle. There is extreme danger. Your taking things into your own hands—"

"Brought us some results, Langdon. I am more than a simple woman. You knew that when we wed. I run a shipping line. I make decisions for myself and am fully responsible for my own actions. I neither need nor want a father-figure looking over my shoulder—"

The words fired inside him, and he moved, grabbed her, and hauled her against his chest. "Does this feel like some damned father-figure?" he demanded and dropped his head, taking her mouth with heat and fire. His anger, frustration, and abject terror coursing hot through his veins.

He savaged her mouth, forcing her to open to him, to give him what he demanded, and the sound of her mewling as he feasted upon her dragged him back to reality.

"I beg your pardon." He fought to control the disgust he felt at himself for the loss of control.

"Langdon?" Her hand cupped his cheek. "You have nothing to beg forgiveness for," she whispered.

God help him, the gentleness of her voice and touch almost undid him. "I do. I should not have grabbed you in anger."

Remorse filled him. He wasn't an ape. He knew Isabelle was a strong-minded woman, but to behave as he did? That proved him far more primitive than he had ever considered.

He pulled away. "I was furious with you, Isabelle, but more than that, I feared for you. I know the dangers and that you only wish to assist, but some things you cannot do." When Isabelle opened her mouth, he shook his head. "Not because you are weak, but because you are a woman. You are strong, but they are men. We've already seen that they hunt in packs. The attack on Staindhouse had to have involved more than one man. Stubens inspected the body, and he's determined there were multiple people. Someone held him. There are marks on his wrists. Someone beat him, the imprints of feet and hands mottle the body. The killing blow though came from behind. It was hard. Delivered by a hammer or some such implement. It must have been wielded by a man to inflict such damage."

Now she quieted, settling into a chair. "How he must have suffered," she mused. Her emotions played over her face: sadness followed by resolution. She nodded as if some internal dialogue took place, and he wondered what rattled around inside her mind. "I have names for you, Langdon. A Mr. Tang and a Mr. Hooper. I was going to ask Mei what her father's surname is, in case he is the Mr. Hooper I was told about."

Langdon cocked his head. "Hooper? Tang? I'm sure I know those names." He tried to remember where he'd heard of them, but his mind was a tangle. He jotted the names down and resolved to check with Stubens on the morrow. For now, he'd focus on the fact that Isabelle had returned, whole and in one piece.

⁂

*I*sabelle waited until the bath had been removed before turning around to pierce Mei with a sharp gaze. "Mei, what is your father's name?"

The girl started, eyes wide and mouth slightly open, clearly discomforted at the question. "Why do you ask?"

She looked at the girl, usually so quiet and meek. Isabelle smiled. "I was hoping you'd tell me so I'd know what name to place on the manifest," she added, hopeful Mei would ask very few questions. While the answer wasn't untrue, it also didn't tell the whole truth. If Mei's father was indeed Hooper, Isabelle planned to pass the information on to Langdon.

"His name is Arnold," the girl answered, dropping her head.

Isabelle contained the sigh that rose. This isn't going to be simple. "Arnold what?"

The girl looked at her, tears welling in the corners of her eyes. "Please, don't ask me," she purred, but Isabelle needed to know.

"His last name, please, Mei."

"Hooper, Mrs. Devereaux. Arnold Hooper." Mei looked so dejected that for a moment, Isabelle knew a sense of disquiet, but she brushed it away.

Hooper! She'd been right. She'd also bet Mei know who Tang was as well, but some deep sense of dread told Isabelle not to push the girl. Not now. The time for further questioning would come. Langdon, however, would no doubt appreciate the information she had to impart.

Instead, she gave instructions for Mei to clear away the clothing she'd discarded and gazed at herself in the mirror.

For the first time in months, she felt satisfaction at her reflection. Her golden hair had grown, and while she'd probably never wear it as long as she had, it glowed in the light. Her body had resumed its pre-illness voluptuousness.

Isabelle ran a hand down her belly, wondering for the first time what it would feel like full and swollen with a babe. Langdon's babe.

She'd never before hoped for such a wonder, yet she was married when just this Christmas past she'd been dejected, sure it would never happen for her.

The wonder of Langdon's love for her had changed her life. The peace and contentment, the miracle of his loving. It all coalesced inside her, and she understood finally. What she felt, the emotions that roiled, had also been love.

"I do. I love him," she whispered. The knowledge wasn't a bolt of lightning, more a gentle warmth that enveloped. "I shall tell him tonight."

She whirled away from the looking glass and headed to the door. It opened beneath her touch, and she stepped into Langdon's embrace.

"You look well this evening, wife."

"As do you, husband. I am ready, as you can see."

His gaze roamed over her form, the bustle tightly pulling the material of her gown back so her figure was displayed. "Indeed, you are." The heat in his eyes and the subtle change of pitch in his voice left her nerves singing with awareness. "We had best leave now, or we shan't go."

Isabelle grabbed her gloves, wrap, and evening bag from the table by the door, and they descended the stairs, her arm wrapped in his.

There was silence between them, not the 'I don't know what to say' variety, but rather a companionable 'we belong together' sort.

They exited the house, climbed into the carriage, and it lurched forward. In the darkness, she felt him shift beside her. "I wonder, if we pulled the curtains, no one could see. Perhaps..." His voice trailed off, but he'd already entranced her with his words.

"Langdon, surely not?"

His bark of laughter echoed inside her. "I have met those who claim it is more than possible. We could, perhaps in warmer weather, investigate?"

Visions of them, daylight dappling through the curtains and he and her naked and entwined. "Oh my..." She had to fan herself at the sudden heat that flared. "Perhaps we could discuss this later. I have plans."

"Tell me more," he urged, but she shook her head with a laugh.

"Not now. Later." She infused the words with every bit of sensuality that she could muster.

"I look forward to it," he answered as the carriage came to a stop.

They waited, the door opened, and they stepped down. Tonight was an informal dinner with several of Langdon's counterparts at the municipal council, and while they'd both agreed that it was important they continued the deception of his role, they also didn't intend to remain longer than necessary.

They entered the residence and met with and conversed with the others, though the chatter was dry.

Dinner was served shortly after that, and the conversation turned to the usual discussions of dinner—the rebellion of the boxers and the after-effects, issues with trade.

The woman to Isabelle's left leaned in. "I hear you participate in trade," she whispered. "How do you cope with all the burly men on the wharf?" She was in the region of her fifth decade, well-preserved though a little faded, her hair streaked liberally with silver.

Isabelle turned. "I'm not sure I understand your meaning, Mrs. Colchrane."

The woman simpered. "Of course you do. Those lovely men with bulging muscles." Awareness flooded Isabelle, and it turned her stomach.

"Mrs. Colchrane, I have no interest in—"

"Pshaw! Of course you do. That's what we Shanghailanders love to hear about."

Isabelle reared away. "If you'll excuse me." She pushed away from the table, capturing Langdon's gaze, and he frowned. She retreated to the retiring room, hoping the horrible woman wouldn't follow her as she regained her equilibrium. "Repulsive woman!" she muttered, washing out her mouth as a bitter taste had settled there. Her inferences that Isabelle might dally with the workers revolted her.

She left the room, and jumped with shock to find Langdon waiting. "What's wrong?" he asked.

Shaking her head, Isabelle wondered if they could somehow excuse themselves, then realized to do so would create more problems for Langdon. "I'm just feeling a trifle unwell," she murmured, and his gaze narrowed.

"What's amiss?"

"We should go back." She tried to step around her husband, but he caught her arm.

"No. What did the woman say to you?"

She blinked. "Really, we should return to the—"

"Mrs. Deveraux, are you unwell?" Their hostess sailed into the small hallway, and she had no choice but to smile.

"I'm—"

"She's feeling a trifle under the weather. The malaria affects her at odd times, so we must beg your pardon," Langdon offered, cutting off Isabelle's answer.

The woman became solicitous. "Of course. Malaria is such a problem in these areas. Go home and rest, Mrs. Deveraux. I'll have your wrap brought through and will make your farewells."

Their hostess ushered them to the front door, instructed the maid to retrieve their coats, and they were both settled back in the carriage before Isabelle could draw a deep breath. In the dark, Langdon tugged her tight against his chest. "What did the old bat say to you?"

She heard the thread of fury. "She suggested I might have been engaged with some of the men on the wharf. Langdon, I wouldn't ever—"

His muscles tensed. "I know you wouldn't. Remember? I'm the first man to have touched you. But that woman has no morals. Her personal exploits are well-known. Colchrane is a good man, but the woman hampers him. Sent here from

England because she engaged in activity a little too openly. Most people bear with her for his sake."

He might say the words, she thought, but it still hurt to be accused of infidelity. Her hand burrowed into his. "I would never..." She gulped, wondering how to explain. "I have no interest in anyone else. I love you."

She heard his tightly indrawn breath. The whoosh of air as he released it. "Good," was all he offered.

Biting her lip, she glanced out the window, avoiding any further discussion, because his light acceptance of her protestations wasn't quite what she'd hoped for. She'd rather he'd given in to some emotional response.

They rounded the corner and arrived home, and they left the carriage in time to see a horseman come flying up the drive.

Langdon thrust her behind him, but the rider came to a stop and handed over a message. With a frown, her husband reached into his pocket, withdrew a coin, and handed it to the rider. Then he dragged her inside.

He tore at the paper, his gaze darkening as he read whatever was written there. "I have to go out," he said and headed for the stairs. "I'll change. See Mrs. Hargraves, have her send for Stubens and horses. Make sure Stubens knows we must go to the alehouse nearest Woosung Road station and sends men." He took the steps two at a time and disappeared before she could gather her wits.

"So much for tonight's plans," she muttered but nonetheless headed to the back of the house as he'd requested.

Stubens was waiting, and they quickly mounted the horses the driver had arranged for them.

"What did you hear?" Stubens demanded as they headed to the tavern Langdon had received the summons to.

"We have a lead on the opium trade. The note just said the contact would be at the alehouse. He's the one who set up the attack on the warehouse. He's been acting as the lynchpin for the information trafficking too."

"Seems convenient, doesn't it?"

Langdon considered Stubens's comment. "Yes, but any lead right now is a start. You've got your men heading there?"

"My best. There will be surveillance until we arrive, then the men will protect our backs once we enter."

Langdon grunted and urged his mount to a faster run. His gut warned him this would not be an easy interview.

The horses were panting by the time they arrived. Langdon and Stubens dismounted, and one of Stubens's men stepped out of the shadows. "Sir, things have been quiet, but a steady stream of Russians has been arriving. We've been keeping an eye out, but so far nothing has occurred."

Langdon wanted to curse. With the Russians there, things would be tense, even though this was technically the outskirts of the English concession. If they also knew who he was, it would tip them off.

"Give me your jacket and hat," he demanded from the younger man.

He looked as if Langdon had run mad. "What? Uh, sir?"

"I can't let them know who I am. Your jacket and cap." He reached down and scooped up some mud, thankful for the darkness so he couldn't see what it was, and smeared it on his face, hands, and streaked it down his pants. He thrust his own jacket to the man and admonished him to keep hold of it.

He and Stubens entered the alehouse, the lights dim, the thick smoke hanging in the air from pipes and the clang of tankards. They took up position at a corner table of the room.

Sinking down to sit on the wooden stools, their backs against the wall, they waited.

A woman, slight with the dark hair of a Chinese woman,

made her way over and bowed deeply. "You like?" she questioned, and Langdon's stomach lurched.

"No, thank you," he answered, but her mouth tightened.

"You want. Say yes," she urged, eyes narrowing as she passed a note surreptitiously to Langdon.

He took it, unfolded it below the top of the table, and exhaled. "Yes."

She sat, taking the spot on the long stool nearest to him. "Pretend you're about to kiss me," she hissed, and he couldn't ignore Stubens's surprise.

He kicked the man under the table and leaned in.

"Hooper is the man you want. He sells women and information. I've seen it. He works from the back room of Tang's Laundry. But beware, Tang is Triad."

That froze the marrow in Langdon's bones. Triad. A secret society known for its brutality. If the Triad were indeed involved, then the danger had become extreme. "What is Tang's involvement?"

The girl spoke very quietly. "He is the one who facilitates the opium and girls. He's a local leader but not the most important. Hooper is merely the face of the slavery. He's coming over now."

"How much for your company, for both of us?" he asked. Langdon knew it was essential to make it look like he wished to procure the girl for sex.

The man, Hooper, slid in beside the girl. His meaty hand settled on her thigh, and he slid it up and down, dislodging her gown, revealing her legs. "She's comely, eh?"

Langdon's stomach churned. He didn't want to do this, but he needed the information. "Indeed. We require a location."

"Ahh, I got me a room. Back of the laundry. You can take her there, for a fee."

Langdon waited, and the man named a sum. He and

Stubens rose, his hand diving into his pocket and withdrawing the amount, which Hooper took gleefully.

It was all too easy, thought Langdon. Far too simple and easy. It could be a trap.

The girl stood, waiting meekly as Hooper made way for her to follow. "She'll take you there and into a pleasure such as you've never known," Hooper boasted.

Langdon hoped that by accessing the room, they might find some information that would implicate this dirty, little man and his trade in women and opium.

They followed the girl, called Jin Yun, as she made her way to the filthy room. He held up a finger to his lips, indicating she should be quiet, and Stubens and he checked the room. Every now and again either of the men would emit a grunt, and he'd shove the pallet on the floor, hoping that should anyone be listening they might think they were taking their pleasure in the girl.

They moved quickly, but with a mission to find anything useful. There were indications of the use of the room, the residue of opium resin smeared the table, and a message slipped into a drawer, its seal broken.

Langdon scanned it then slid it into his pocket. The information contained within indicated that the recipient would be receiving payment for the 'eradication of a problem,' and later the name Staindhouse was crossed out.

Finally satisfied they'd gathered the information they required, they mussed their clothes and wordlessly instructed the girl to do so as well. Langdon pulled the girl close and gave her the direction of his home. "When it's safe, go there. You will be protected, I promise."

Jin Yun blinked and nodded slowly. It was the best any of them could do right now.

Then Langdon jerked the door open and emerged to find Hooper sitting on a chair waiting. "Enjoyed her, did you?

She's well broken in now, but if you're looking for more action, I have a new girl coming in soon."

The vicious gleam in Hooper's eyes turned Langdon's stomach.

Stubens stepped up. "We'll be in touch soon to find out more." His quick thinking saved Langdon from the necessity of coming up with some suitable lie.

The man grinned and rubbed his hands together. "Nice doing business, sirs."

They retreated, the sounds and stench of stale sex high in the air. He didn't breathe deeply again until they were riding away, aware that they could be followed. The letter in his pocket and what they'd seen was enough to ensure Hooper would be arrested.

Near his home, Langdon pulled up, and they led the horses into the dark gap between two buildings at the edge of the French concession. Waiting.

If there were any rear attack, this would be the time and the place, surmised Langdon.

Time passed and one, two, then a third Chinese man made his way down the street. Clothing dark, they denoted the men who would assassinate those who crossed them.

They moved forward, seeking Langdon and Stubens, who waited in the dark, calming their horses until it was safe to emerge.

Time passed, and slowly they led their horses out and headed for Langdon's home. In his mind, he wondered how best to fortify the property without it seeming obvious. How could he protect Isabelle?

He'd guessed there was some association with the Triad but didn't expect it would run so deep.

"Come in," he said to Stubens when they arrived at the house. He led the man to the library, then reached into his pocket and pulled out the message.

Payment will be forwarded to you tomorrow. Your work ensuring eradication of the problem is noted. Lay low and don't show interest in the Staindhouse matter.
Tang Bao

"He's implicated with the letter," crowed Stubens.

"Maybe. Or it's a plant. Either way, we have to get this information to the consul, and we need the constables to act swiftly."

Stubens nodded. "I'll take this then."

Langdon would have preferred to hold onto the letter, but it needed to be admitted as evidence. "Bury it deep until we need it," he urged.

The man took his leave, and Langdon poured himself a glass of whiskey, needing a moment before he could go upstairs and bathe. A moment to push away the knowledge of the uses of the girls in Hooper's clutches. When Jin Yun arrived, he planned to find out how many more there were, and where they were stashed. Perhaps, once Hooper was in custody, they could free the girls.

It wouldn't fix the issue. He knew they'd never return home. They were stained and unclean because they'd been used as prostitutes, but perhaps he could give them the chance of a better future. How he honestly didn't know. But he'd do what he could.

Langdon drained the glass, left it on the desk, and rose. At the top of the stairs, he stopped, his gaze settling on Isabelle's door. He couldn't go into her yet, not smelling of the laundry.

He strode along the hall and entered his chamber then halted, surprised to see Isabelle waiting for him.

She came forward, eyes hooded, garbed in only a thin, lacey confection with a light silk chemise beneath it. She reached up on tiptoe as if to launch herself into his embrace, then stilled.

She reared away, her mouth hanging open, eyes startled

and wide. "Smell," she whispered, and his heart plummeted to his stomach.

"Isabelle, it's not what it seems." He reached for the bell pull and summoned Fuchs who hurried into the room.

Isabelle watched, her face pale, lips trembling as he demanded a bath and hot water.

Fresh clothes.

Fuchs looked from him to Isabelle and back again then hurried out.

"Where have you been?" The strangled sound of her words left him tense.

"I had to go to an alehouse and meet Stubens. We had a lead to follow. It led to a girl." She closed her eyes, hand sliding to her mouth.

"She had information, but nothing took place, Isabelle. Once I've bathed, I'll explain it all."

She tottered to the bed, eyes now open and settled on him, tears glistening. "Nothing happened?"

He shook his head. "No. Nothing could. I told you, I love you. This is a messy situation though, and sometimes things will happen, things that I can't easily explain away, but you have to trust me."

It was hard to consider they'd known each other barely seven weeks, had been married for just over three, but at the heart of it, they still had much to learn about each other. He just hoped she'd accept, once he explained, that it had been necessary.

The bath came in, Fuchs and the men left, and he stripped now, aware that the entire time Isabelle was watching in silence.

"I want to. I mean, I do. It's just you smell of other women."

He lathered and rinsed, considering how to explain. "I had to meet a woman called Jin Yun. She gave me the opportunity to meet with Hooper."

Isabelle let out a squeak. "Arnold Hooper? Mei's father?"

He stopped, considered her words. "It would be the same person, yes. He's keeping girls captive."

She nodded. "Mei's father. She said he had slaves. Girls. So, what else?"

"He's also involved in the opium trade. We found evidence in the room where he sends clients with girls. I believe he also was involved in Staindhouse's death."

Isabelle straightened up on the bed. "Then he must pay."

Convinced he'd washed away the evidence of his time in the dingy room, he rose, water sliding from his skin, and he accepted the towel Isabelle extended to him.

"I agree, however, he's also involved with the Triad and possibly even the Russians."

His wife screwed up her nose. "What is the Triad?"

He rubbed and considered the best way to describe them. "They are a group of people who band together. They were involved in many things, including the opium trade, prostitution, and we believe were involved in the riots that took place outside Shanghai in the last little while. They're dangerous. Will do whatever it takes, kill whoever they need to eliminate to protect themselves and their evil trade."

"Are you in danger?" Isabelle asked, and he stopped, considering her query.

"Possibly, but so are you, Isabelle. You mustn't leave here without letting me know. Please."

He opened his arms, dropping the towel, and she slid into his embrace, and he sighed. The feel of her scantily clad body against his naked skin was reassuring as much as it was arousing. Reality intruded faintly.

"I know this is all seems to be a lot to take in right now," he said. "But I have to keep you safe."

The way she nestled into his arms allayed his fears. But there would be more danger. More things that might happen that would cause them unrest before this case was done.

In that instant, he knew this would be the last investigation he would undertake for the crown. He wanted more. A family. His wife. The danger he'd faced regularly no longer spurred him on. He'd not endanger what they had and what they could have.

Langdon lifted her, and she squeaked. He strode to the connecting door and nudged it open while Isabelle wound her arms around his neck.

Once within her boudoir, he kicked the door closed and allowed her to slide to the floor, before the full-length looking glass.

"Come," he said and gestured for her to stand in front of it. "Let me show you the true gift we share."

Her gaze followed his in the glass, sapphire watching him.

His fingers found the ribbon closure of her robe and released the tie. With careful and slow movements, he reached up and slid the robe from her shoulders. "See how I worship you with my hands." He reached around and cupped her breasts through the light silk, the outline of her nipples jutting against the material. If he looked carefully, the strawberry pink of them showed through the light material. "When I look at you, I see femininity. I can spy the outline through the cloth, and it makes me hard, Isabelle. Feel how I push against you." He slid his hips forward so the hardness of his erection nudged at her buttocks. "Do you? Can you feel me?" he whispered against her throat.

Her eyes glittered, and she licked her lips. "I... Yes, Langdon."

"Tell me how you feel, *ma belle*."

"I'm hot. I feel like my skin is ready to burst. Deep inside, I feel heat and want."

Such a sensual creature his wife was. He burned too. Wanted deeply. His pleasure would wait a while yet, he reminded himself.

With unsteady fingers, he found the tiny buttons on her

shoulders that held her gown closed. He flicked them, and the gown slid down. He was baring her to their gazes. Langdon held her still, keeping her in place even though she squirmed. He might be naked and his body heavy with desire, but he'd pleasure her first. Make her burn, then he'd start all over again.

"See how our bodies are different. You're soft. Your breasts are perfect. They fit into the palms of my hands." He captured one breast with his hand, the darkness of his sun-darkened skin contrasting against the milky white flesh. "Your body knows I want you. See how your nipple hardens?" He slipped a finger over it, and she arched into him. He laughed his pleasure at the way she responded to his caresses.

He slid the other hand around her waist, splaying his hand and pulling her closer against him. She quivered, and he bent down, captured the long sweep of her neck in a kiss. His teeth grazed the sensitive skin, and she moaned.

"Keep watching, *ma belle*. See what I do next," he whispered. His hunger was urgent, and he knew she knew it too as she moved restlessly against his head. His hand slipped, finding the thatch of curls covering her mons. "Such a beautiful woman. All mine."

"Langdon?" she mewled, "this isn't seemly."

He laughed. "Our rules."

Langdon reached down and tipped her head back so he could feast upon her lips. They opened and she met him, caress for caress, their tongues tangling.

She turned into his embrace, and he hauled her close, glorying in the sensation of his naked skin rubbing against her.

When they parted, she gulped a lung full of oxygen. His gaze traveled down her body, and he dropped himself to the floor.

"Langdon?"

"Shhh," he whispered, winding his arms around her hips.

He nuzzled at her, the junction of her thighs at the level of his lips. Langdon leaned in, touching the pearl hidden from view with the tip of his tongue.

"Ohhhh..." moaned Isabelle.

With slow moves, he parted her legs and rubbed the sensitive nub again. "Do you feel me tasting you, Isabelle? You're like the finest honey. Now watch."

Her essence coated his tongue, and he fed now, rapacious as she wavered, her nails digging deep and tugging him up.

He gave in and rose, letting the tips of her nipples scrape against his sensitized flesh. When their lips met, he slid his tongue deep, then tugged away. "Taste yourself on my mouth."

They kissed again, this time slower, more a caress of lips, then he turned her so she faced the looking glass once more.

"Watch me love you, *ma belle*," he urged and slid his hand down so it burrowed between her silken thighs. "See how I glory in your body." With a soft, gentle movement, he slid a finger within her, then raised his eyes so their gazes met. "See?"

She writhed in his arms. "Langdon? More!"

He pulled away, his chest bellowing with exertion. "Now I'm going to fill you."

He bent her over his arm, her breasts sliding wantonly as he positioned himself behind her. "Feel me," he muttered and guided the now distended head of his cock at her entrance, fingers parting her further and playing as he slid deep.

She cried out, a screaming moan of pleasure, and he moved, rocking back and forth, loving the way she slid against him, meeting his thrusts. "Please Langdon," she implored, sliding her hand behind to haul him closer.

He could feel the powerful drag of Isabelle's muscles then the explosion of her orgasm. It milked him, urged, and finally, he came, emptying, lost in the wonder of the woman in his arms. When it was done, they dropped slowly to the floor, and he held her against his chest, his breath coming in pants. "I love you, *ma belle*," he whispered.

"*Je t'aime*," she answered.

He smiled. "You remembered."

"You use French when you're...engaged," she answered.

"Indeed, I do, *ma belle*." On shaking legs, he rose and lifted her into his arms. "Come. To bed, wife."

Chapter Sixteen

____

THE NEXT MORNING, Isabelle rose to a commotion. She dragged on her nightgown, the one Langdon had conveniently left on the end of the bed, and climbed from the bed. Mei entered the room, Mrs. Hargraves following swiftly behind.

"Forgive the intrusion, Mrs. Deveraux," the older woman said. "There's a Jin Yun here to see Mr. Deveraux, but he's left for the office."

Isabelle glanced at the clock and was horrified to see the time was well after ten in the morning. "Oh, well..."

"Mrs. Deveraux, she is unclean. Cannot be here," uttered Mei, her face a mask of dismay.

Isabelle struggled as the accent from the girl was quite pronounced this morning. "Unclean?"

"She one of my father's girls."

It took a moment for understanding to dawn. Oh! A sex slave! "Oh, dear. Mrs. Hargraves, you should send for my husband," she said then turned to Mei. "I need to dress. Keep the girl downstairs until either of us is available, Mrs. Hargraves," she mumbled and waited for the woman to leave then she dragged off the nightgown as Mei rushed about finding clothing suitable for at home. Not that she'd be taking visitors today, she decided.

Once in a tidy brown dress, her hair brushed and tied back in a simple chignon, Isabelle hurried down the stairs, just as her husband entered the house. "Where is she?" he asked, and Isabelle frowned.

"Likely the kitchen."

They stepped into the room at the rear of the house together to see a Chinese girl waiting, her face a mass of bruises and her gown torn. She looked from Isabelle to Langdon, tears rolling down her face.

"Tang's men came in the night. They took him outside and beat me. When they left, I waited then went out. He's dead." The words tumbled out, and Isabelle turned to Langdon, seeking clarification.

"Hooper? He's dead?"

Isabelle felt ill at Langdon's words. If Hooper was dead, then what did that mean for Mei? For the investigation into the death of Staindhouse? "Langdon?"

He shook his head and turned to Mrs. Hargraves. "Send someone for Stubens." Then he turned to her. "Go get Mei."

Isabelle scurried out to collect the girl and bring her back into the kitchen with her.

Langdon sat on a seat beside Jin Yun, asking questions. "Where are the other girls?"

She shook her head, but Mei advanced, said something in staccato Chinese to Jin Yun, then turned back. "I told her I know and would tell you. She's afraid. The Triad might try to hurt her." She spoke again, rapid-fire. "They are kept in a shack on the edge of the Yang-tzu Chiang. I know where and can take you there. But Jin Yun is right. The Triad is dangerous. You must use great care, because losing these girls will mean they will lose coin and face. This is very bad."

"Mei, he was your father, right?" Mei nodded, and for a moment, Isabelle felt some small comfort. "Then at least you're free of him." But Mei didn't show any excitement or enthusiasm. "Mei? You'll come with us to England."

Langdon pushed up to his feet and stalked the length of the room and back. "With Hooper dead, we don't have much to go on. Thanks to the letter we found, we know Tang is the lynchpin."

Isabelle couldn't contain her shock. "Letter?"

"I'll explain later." Then he continued his pacing. "Where does the connection to Tang take us?"

Jin Yun shuddered. "The Russians."

Everyone turned and stared at the girl. "The Russians?" parroted Langdon.

"We are used sometimes to collect information from the Russians. They send letters on the ships. To England and other countries. They want to control the opium trade, and we are sent to the wharves to comfort the men. There are some on the ships who would collect letters or send them."

Isabelle closed her eyes. Send letters. Collect them. Her captains did, from time to time, carry intelligence for the navy and government. She'd learned of that while in India. She also knew that there were some Englishmen who'd sold out to the Russians in the hopes they'd be rewarded. Could that be part of the plot? If so, how the hell could they possibly form a plan to trick them into showing their hand?

The reality was, she was in over her head, and likely so too was Langdon. It was a cold dousing of fact. "Langdon, may I have a word?" He followed her over to the corner of the kitchen. "What are we going to do?"

He glanced at her, his gaze steady. "We're going to find whoever is behind this plot, and we're going to neutralize them once and for all. Then you and I are going home. Back to England."

She blinked. This wasn't quite the answer she'd expected. Indeed, she wasn't sure she liked the idea that he'd suddenly demand she accede to all his requests. "Langdon? I have things to do—"

His hand cupped her face. "I know. We'll find a new man of business for you, we'll source what you need, but then we return home. I'm planning to hand in my commission." Now he turned away, scratched his head, and appeared deep in thought.

The back door to the kitchen opened and in strode Stubens and his three young constables. "Guv?"

"Hooper is dead. Tang's men and the Triad were behind it. We've got girls to free, the Triad members to find and prosecute, and the Russians too."

Stubens gave him a 'you can't be serious' stare, and Isabelle waited for the fraught moment to pass. "Have you given this much thought?" Stubens enquired.

"Not yet. It needs some consideration, but overall, that's what must happen," Langdon answered, and Isabelle tottered to a seat and dropped into it.

"Langdon? How do you plan to help the girls? If Mei's reaction is anything to go by, they aren't going to be able to go home and live as they did before."

He shook his head. "No. I think there are opportunities in America or England. We find them employment. Some places specialize in helping girls. It's not ever going to be perfect, but at least they'd have hope."

Isabelle pursed her lips. Forster Shipping would be able to assist if this was what Langdon wanted. "Fine. I'm sure I can make a provision for their transport. We'd need more definite plans, but that doesn't address everything."

"I need time to think," he answered. "But before we do anything else, we need to get the girls, before the Triad members can take them and hand them to someone else. Mei?"

The girl sat up straight. "I can ride," she stated. "I can show you."

If Mei could show them, and on horseback, then so too would Isabelle. "I'm coming with you."

Langdon and Stubens both looked aghast at her announcement, but she raised her chin.

"The girls may not come with Mei if there is only one woman. We'll need a way to transport them. You can't make them walk and—"

"I'll arrange transport," muttered Stubens, and he beat a hasty retreat from the room.

"Mei, do you have suitable clothing?" Isabelle refused to allow the girl to embarrass herself. If necessary, she was sure there was a gown in her trunks that would fit the bill.

"I go as I am. Anything else would tell the girls to be worried."

She wanted to remonstrate, but Langdon nodded. "That makes sense. Mei, go prepare while I talk to my wife."

Mrs. Hargraves slid a bowl of soup in front of the woman who'd brought about this situation.

Langdon steered Isabelle through to the hall. "If you come, there will be danger. Do you know how to shoot?"

Another facet of her that he hadn't yet seen, she thought. "I do. I'm quite a shot, Langdon, and I do have a small pistol in my trunk. I'll change and bring it down with me."

He looked so uncertain that she raised herself onto tiptoes and kissed him softly on the lips.

"Remember, I'm no meek princess who's lived in a gilded cage, my love. I run a shipping line, and sometimes our vessels get stopped. A woman must always be able to defend herself, even on a ship." She caressed his cheek. "Now, let me go change while you plan."

They rode in silence, a posse of fifteen, a covered wagon at the center and Mei up front beside Isabelle. It wasn't quite what Langdon had expected, the trip slow and tortuous. The entire time, his mind played over all the myriad things that might go wrong. The girls already gone. Mei leading them into a trap—not that he actually believed that to be the case. Isabelle taking some chance and not surviving. That was his greatest fear.

At the edge of the water, he stopped, the cabin in full view. Two of the constables flanked Mei, and they rode forward slowly while the rest of the party prepared for the worst and hoped for the best.

Isabelle and Langdon followed, slower, and looking for any hint of danger.

Mei dismounted and opened the door, peered inside, then signaled the two constables to enter. The door closed behind the three who'd entered the structure.

Moments slid by sluggish, and Langdon waited, his heart beating rapidly, Isabelle at his side.

The door opened again, the young constable waving them forward, and they called for the others to join them—the pumping of Langdon's heart a tattoo of fear in his bloodstream.

He and Isabelle dismounted and entered the cabin. It was dingy. Dark. Several women were chained to the walls, faces black with dirt, and more than one moaning in discomfort. Mei moved around unshackling the women and urging them upright. She spoke urgently, and obediently they rose as the last was released.

Isabelle bit her lip as she inspected the women. "At least one is expecting, Langdon."

He didn't have the heart to tell her that some men would pay a premium for an expecting woman. Instead, he grunted and urged them to the door. The dray pulled up, and the women climbed aboard, Mei joining them as they'd agreed. The door was fastened, and a covering draped over the women who crouched beneath it. Out of sight was out of mind, Langdon thought.

"Let's get out of here," Stubens said.

In the short time, they'd been in the shack, Langdon had made a quick study, noting there was nowhere to hide letters or contraband. No, if there was more evidence, he was sure it wasn't here.

He wanted to growl with frustration, but now wasn't the time. Instead, the entourage kept steady time, moving as swiftly as they dared until they reached their location—the Shanghai municipal council building.

The group called a halt. The cover pulled back from the women, where they hunched. Mei took the reins of her horse back from Isabelle, it having been decided that the men would be better suited to the safety of the women, and Isabelle proved a better than mediocre horse-woman anyway.

The horses were taken into the stables out back, and Langdon helped Isabelle down from the saddle. "Well," she said, carefully rubbing at her back, "it's been too long since I've ridden."

He ushered her and the other women inside, and they trailed to his small office. He'd reasoned keeping them together meant they'd feel a whole lot more comfortable. The six women banded together, and only Jin Yun seemed willing to talk.

"Jin Yun, can you tell us where you were abducted from?" He directed his question to Mei, aware the woman wouldn't trust anyone else at this point to translate. He knew she understood and spoke some English, but it was vitally important that they have the whole story. Without errors.

They chattered away, and Mei sighed. "She's from upper Yang-tzu Chiang."

While Mei had questioned her, Langdon had pulled out a

map. They made a note on the location, and he had Mei ask the other women. They came from a range of locations. More than one, two, and three days ride away.

"Ask them how it happened," he instructed Mei, and she asked them.

"They were walking along, carrying items for their families, or heading out to harvest. It was always a group of three or four men. They'd bind them and stop them from talking by putting things over their mouths. Then they'd lift them onto horses and bring them to that hut. Some have only been there a short time. Some longer. Jin Yun, years. She knew my mother and was there when she died."

The girl spoke in the wooden fashion of someone who had just heard something horrendous about themselves. Later, he'd ask her. For now, he focused on the task of finding a safe shelter for the women, and the one Isabelle was sure was expecting would need to be checked by a physician.

One of the constables lived with his mother, and they sent for her. He'd assured them his mother sometimes took in fosterlings. This was a little different, but if they could safely house the women until Isabelle could arrange their transportation that would be best.

"Mrs. Carver is here, Major," his assistant intoned, his face tight with disapproval, but Langdon waved the man aside and opened the door for the massive, blunt-faced woman.

Her gaze took in the women, and she frowned. "This them? The poor lambs. I'll take them, and no one will get past my Freddy and me."

The constable frowned. "Ma," he remonstrated, but she bussed him on the arm.

"Hush now. Let's see. One is expecting. Is she the only one?"

Mei shook her head and pointed to Jin Yun.

"Right, home we go. A nice warm bath and some food. We'll need clothes, Major," she tutted, and he smiled, comforted by the matronly way the woman was talking to the girls.

Jin Yun chattered to the girls and told them what happened, he guessed, as they looked fearful, shoulders hunched and eyes downcast. Mei entered the discussion, and he waited for her to indicate they were ready to leave.

"I'll have my dressmaker round up appropriate clothing," Isabelle said as she slumped into the chair, her face drawn, and eyes closed after the room had emptied.

"This wasn't too much for you?"

She opened her eyes and glanced at him. "No. It's the knowledge that someone would do this to the women. They aren't commodities to be bought and sold."

He read both frustration and anger in her voice.

"I feel helpless. Someone should be helping them, but all we're doing is providing emergency care. They need more. They deserve more." Her eyes welled with tears. "I want to do more for them, Langdon."

He understood her emotions. "When we return to England, perhaps we can. There will always be a trade like this. We could help the girls..."

Isabelle scrubbed at her cheeks. "Why should we wait?"

He crouched down before her and took her hands in his. He willed her to understand. "I would, but my role right now is to find the people who are trafficking in both information and women. The opium suppliers. That means I must give my attention to that. I need you to stay safe, which means curtailing your trips."

She cracked open her eyes. "I won't stay at home."

Now his anger took over. "You will remain at home unless I'm with you."

Isabelle rose up, her face a mask of fury. "I'm in control of my own life."

"Damn it, Isabelle, see reality. You're a target. You go out there, unguarded, and they'll have you dead so fast you won't even feel it when you hit the floor!"

She pushed him back as he stood. "Don't tell me what to do, Langdon Deveraux. I'm not a lapdog."

Isabelle spun away, headed for the door, and he watched as the pressure in his head grew. If only he could make her understand.

Her hand curled around the knob of his office door. "I will do what's best of Forster Shipping and me," she hurled at him and was out of the office.

She'll be back in a moment, once she's worked off the first blush of her mad, he told himself as he watched the door. One moment passed, then another.

Any moment, he told himself. But she didn't return.

His fury melted, replaced by the frigid wash of fear that iced his bones. Now he followed her path to the door.

"Mrs. Deveraux left the building, sir," his assistant commented, and Langdon hurried to the front of the office building. When he reached it, there was no sign of her.

She's either gone home or to the warehouse, he thought and gathered his men. Sent them looking though he remained behind in case she returned.

Stubens returned first. "She's not at the warehouse."

When Martin arrived with the same news from the house, his gut clenched tight. The message arrived, carried by a young Chinese girl.

We have your wife.
We know more about your investigation than you think.
Return the women, and we'll restore your wife to you.
You have one day.

Though it was unsigned, he knew the handwriting. Tang.

Chapter Seventeen

ISABELLE FOUGHT the bonds that felt like they tightened with every twist. Her wrists burned, and her temper flared. More at herself than the situation. She should have listened to Langdon. He'd been right, and she'd fought against the perceived control he wanted to exert over her. Her temper had overridden good sense.

Now, she was here, in a hovel that reminded her of the place they'd retrieved the women from.

Even worse, she hadn't been aware of her abduction until she'd noticed her carriage was traveling in the wrong direction, and by then it had been too late. She attempted opening the door of the carriage, but they'd locked it from the outside.

"Let me out," she called, but no one answered. Either they didn't understand, couldn't hear, or they just ignored her. Any of those three facts were cause for increased concern.

Isabelle let her gaze roam. The room might be dark, but she'd been here long enough to become accustomed to the dimness.

She could see the building was well-sealed. "At least I won't be overly cold," she muttered, well aware that the late March weather had brought warmer days and nights.

The bonds tying her were rope but felt sturdy and thick. If she lurched forward, they didn't give, so they were well-secured, and she was alone in the dingy room.

She moved her feet, aware not for the first time of the urgent pressure of her bladder. *I've been here a while. Surely, they'll bring me water and let me relieve myself soon.*

As if by magic, a young girl entered the room, a pot in hand. She held it out, and Isabelle wanted to shy away from the stench of it. "Use." The girl shoved it in her direction, and she tried to recoil. "Use," was repeated.

"Please, untie me first," Isabelle said, but the girl looked blankly at her. Isabelle knew then that the girl didn't understand.

Tears of pure fury gathered in her eyes. Such an indignity could scarcely be believed, but the need was urgent, so she let the girl help her to her knees and remove the layers of cloth before she used the pot.

The girl spat in her direction as she left the room, and Isabelle felt heat rise in her face. "I have to get out of here," she told herself and once more began twisting and turning. Whatever it took to escape.

At some point later, another woman, this one older and careworn, entered with a dipper of water. "Drink," she crooned.

Isabelle drank deeply, her mouth parched.

"Let me out," she whispered.

"Soon," the woman whispered, and Isabelle's eyes whipped to the woman. "Your man will pay for your return," she cackled, and the hope that had risen in her chest shriveled.

*L*angdon paced the office. They hadn't found a trace of Isabelle. The carriage driver had been knocked unconscious and dumped. The carriage found some distance away with locks attached to the doors where they hadn't been before.

No one had seen anything untoward.

His men were busy canvassing the alehouses and taverns, the seedy palaces, and even the opium dens.

A knock sounded, and he jerked upright. "Come in," he bellowed, and Mrs. Hargraves, her face pale and drawn, pushed the door wide.

"A woman has a note for you, sir."

He gestured that she be brought before him and in tottered a woman, her age unclear though her face was lined, her teeth blackened, and her form hunched in a stained quipao. "What do you have?"

She smiled. "A lady matching the one you seek is currently held by Tang. If you pay, we will give her to you." Her voice was cultured and soft, but he'd been deceived before.

"How do I know you have her?"

The woman laughed. "Smart you are. Here." She shoved a scrap of lace into his hands. One he knew well—her small bag. Nausea rose from his gut, sharp and bitter.

"She is unharmed?"

The woman nodded. "For now. If Tang comes back, I cannot be sure she will remain so. Fifty guineas." She held out a clawed hand.

"Ten now. Ten when we arrive. The last thirty when she's released." He wouldn't haggle. There would be no use in that. Instead, he'd make sure it wasn't a trick—something to raise his hopes purely to dash them again.

The woman cocked her head. "Fine. You come now."

"Wait! Why? Why are you doing this?"

The crone stared at him. "He's bad for us. Leads badly, and we will die badly if we follow. My man, he better leader. We follow him. Now come."

"Where?" he demanded, and she narrowed her eyes. "I will not follow where my men cannot find me."

The woman shook her head. "No. No men. No follow."

His hand balled, but he reached deep into his pocket and withdrew the purse he secreted. Removed ten, then another ten, and dropped the purse to the table. "The last thirty once we are safely back here."

"No. When we arrive." Then she cackled as if she knew he was hostage to his fears.

"Thirty-five when we arrive back here." A gleam rose in her eyes, and he cursed. He emptied the purse, and a tinkle of coins dropping to the surface filled the air. "This. All of it. When we return."

The woman shrugged. "All. When back here."

She whirled, and he hurried behind her, pushing past an amazed Mrs. Hargraves. "Have Stubens and his men here when I return," he said. All he could do was hope she'd listened as he hurried after the woman.

They moved on foot, taking deserted laneways, dark streets, and emerged at the edge of town, well away from the English concession. He padded on foot across the fields, the ones she led him over as if she traversed them daily.

On the edge of the Chinese village, she stopped at a tiny house. "Shhh..." She skimmed the side of the house, looking into the darkness. "Come," she urged him on, and he entered a courtyard, quiet and empty. They hurried toward a door, and she stopped him. "Stay," she said, and opened the wooden barrier, slid inside.

He craned and waited in the dark, his guts a knot of fear for long minutes. Footsteps, quiet but distinct, caught his attention, and he shrank back into the long shadows of the dark night.

The woman emerged, a shrouded woman following. She came close and whispered to Langdon, "We go quickly now." But before she could tug her prisoner away, Langdon had whipped off the cover.

Isabelle blinked, her face pale and streaked with dirt. She sobbed but quieted when the woman hissed.

Langdon hated to think about what may have happened to her. He lifted her into his arms. She held herself like a statue in his embrace as he followed the woman from the yard. They moved swiftly, keeping to the edges of the fields, mud sloshing and squelching, but Isabelle remained silent.

He hated the knowledge that she'd known fear, but there was naught he could do until she was safely back at the house. They reached the town when a howl went up. "Quickly now," the woman ordered, and he hurried faster behind her, his footsteps loud. The sound of men running through the night filled the air, and the older woman pushed him against a door. "You stay. I go."

She scurried away, and with his heart in his throat, Langdon held Isabelle close as she trembled in silence.

"We're going home, Isabelle," he crooned almost silently against her ear.

It didn't stop the shaking, but she did settle a little.

He waited for the footsteps to die away then headed out, following his internal compass.

Down three lanes then across a darkened street, he stayed to the edges, searching for shadows and places where they might be waylaid. Hours passed as he made his way on the serpentine style route.

Realizing where he was, he stopped outside a small house. Hammered on the door. It opened eventually, and a blinking woman stared at him. "Langdon! Come in. What's..."

He brushed past her, then admonished the woman to quickly bolt the door and extinguish the light, lest it be seen and noted. She dragged him and Isabelle into the heart of the house, and he finally drew in a deep breath. "Justina, pray forgive the intrusion. I'm in trouble and needed assistance."

Justina Elgin blinked. "Of course you should come here. Come, you should put her down and take a moment."

Isabelle quaked harder, and he shook his head. "No. But we do need somewhere to hide until morning. Please."

Justina pursed her lips, thinking as she always did, and ushered them up the stairs, into a small bedroom. The one beside the room where they'd conducted their trysts, and the irony of that wasn't lost on him.

"You'll need water, won't you?" she asked. "And cloths."

He nodded, and she hurried away, returning moments later with the items. He took the items from her hands, then slid them onto the large boxes he'd noted throughout the room— crates for a sea voyage.

"Thank you."

"Your wife, I take it?" she asked, and embarrassment streaked through him.

"Yes." If it weren't for Isabelle, he would have attempted to make it back to the house.

But that fact that she'd been in no fit state to take the chance that she'd remained barely responsive terrified him

"You'll both be safe here," Justina added before pulling the door shut.

He'd laid Isabelle down on the bed, and now he settled his hip on the edge. "Isabelle? *Ma belle*?" He slid a careful hand over her forehead. No fever.

Her lashes fluttered. "Langdon?" Her voice was weak, and his gut clenched. "My head hurts," she whispered, and he reached up, finding a large lump at the back, sticky and matted with hair.

"What happened?"

"He hit me. Wanted to know what we knew. I didn't tell him anything." Through the weakness, he heard a thread of victory. It was heartening, and yet it hurt to know she'd been attacked because she'd kept his confidences.

"Oh, Isabelle." He leaned down, levered her up, and unfastened the remains of her coiffure. Much of the blood was dried. "Did he hit you elsewhere?"

She shrugged. "Not hard." She groaned. "Chest and legs."

He cursed under his breath. He'd make Tang pay for his actions. For now though, he unfastened the gown, grimy and torn, so he could get to where she'd been hurt. There were faint tinges of bruises, and he washed them, promising himself that once they returned home, he'd ensure she rested and recouped her strength.

He tugged the gown back up and settled in beside her, the bowl and cloth forgotten on the dressing table. Holding her close settled the wild thunder of his heart, and not for the first time, he wondered at the wisdom of allowing her to be involved.

Isabelle nestled in, and on a sigh, she settled down. "I was scared," she whispered, "not that I'd die so much, but that I'd tell." Her fingers curled into the material of his jacket. "I won't let you down."

The burn of tears was almost more than he could bear. He blinked but felt the scalding river tracing down his cheeks. "You'd never let me down, *ma belle*." He hauled her closer, needing her to know just how much he'd feared her disappearance. The hunger and need built once more, but he ruthlessly controlled it.

That would wait until they were back at the house and he could take his time. Loving shouldn't be rushed, and she was in no fit state for such embraces anyway. So, he settled down on the narrow bed, holding the woman he adored close, and thanked every deity he could think of for his second chance.

*I*sabelle couldn't say what woke her. It might be the brush of his hair against her forehead. The gentle circles he traced on her back. Whatever it was, she opened her eyes. Her head ached, and she had discomfort from Tang's furious slaps and kicks, but she was awake, and, if she didn't miss her guess, in Langdon's arms.

She blinked. "How did we get here?"

The sigh against her ear was long. "You don't remember last night?"

Shaking her head felt like her brain would rattle, so Isabelle stilled. "Not really. I mean, I remember seeing your face, then it's rather blurred from there. Where are we?"

"At a...friend's house."

She didn't miss the hesitation. It fueled her interest, but for now, she'd be patient. "Are we going back to the house?"

"Soon. Once the sun is higher in the sky and I'm sure Tang's men have dispersed."

Isabelle flinched at his name.

"Tell me what happened?"

"Can we talk later, Langdon. Right now, I want to go home." She scrubbed her hand over her face.

"Then we'll talk then. For now, we should rise. Justina has arranged food downstairs."

"Justina?" Isabelle swung her feet over the side of the bed, wincing as the variety of aches made themselves known.

"Come here," he said, and when she turned, it was to note the crest of embarrassment that tinged his cheeks a bright crimson.

He assisted her back into her torn and stained gown, then she followed him out of the room and down the stairs. At the bottom, he took her hand and guided her into a tiny parlor, where a woman waited. Her eyes were bright, her ebony hair swept up into a basic knot that didn't detract from the long line of her neck. The gown, though plain, accentuated her figure. All this, Isabelle noted in a swift glance.

"You're awake, Mrs. Deveraux. I'm pleased. When Langdon arrived last night—this morning," she amended, "I wasn't sure we shouldn't call for the physician. Anyway, if you'll sit, I've organized a light omelet. Langdon, I've got your favorite ham and eggs." The woman— Justina, Isabelle guessed—bustled about as they took a spot by the fire.

Justina brought the meals then settled in with them, her own repast of toast and tea reminding Isabelle of the differences between herself and this woman.

"So, Langdon, what brought you to my door in the middle of the night?" Justina questioned, and he winced.

"I can't discuss that with you, Justina. As you know, there are things—"

The woman reached out, touched Langdon's arm, and a tiny seed of jealousy rose in Isabelle. She might be his wife, and he'd professed to love her, but the connection between these two was clearly long-standing and allowed for intimacies she found unsettling.

"Of course, Langdon. You're welcome to stay as long as you need to." She nibbled at her toast, watching Isabelle and Langdon.

"We'll be on our way once we've broken our fast. But I do thank you for your hospitality, Justina. Things were..." He paused as if considering what exactly to say. "Things were fraught." He frowned, and Isabelle watched him in silence, noting the hints of emotions warring deeply inside him. "Justina, when do you intend to sail for England?"

Isabelle sat up a little straighter. Was she sailing for England? Surely he had no intention of continuing whatever liaison they'd previously enjoyed on their own return to England? That idea turned her stomach.

"I have purchased a ticket on a ship leaving at the end of the week, and I have someone interested in taking over the house. There is nothing much to keep me here and your funds—"

He shook his head. "Yours, Justina. Your friendship was important to me. Still is. But the sooner you leave, the better." Now, Langdon turned to Isabelle. "One of your ships?"

"I...perhaps." Indeed, she'd need to find a replacement for

Staindhouse soon though, because it was only a matter of weeks before she needed to have the next shipments ready.

Justina narrowed her eyes. "Forster? Miss Forster?"

"Mrs. Deveraux now," answered Langdon, and Justina blushed.

"Of course. Forgive me. I had heard that the Forster ladies were here in Shanghai. That you both own and run the shipping line. It's been the talk of Shanghai for some time."

Isabelle cocked her head to the side. "What else had you heard?"

"Of the incident where your man of business was murdered. Have you made arrangements yet for his replacement?"

"No. I'm not quite sure where to begin. We usually have someone prepared to take over the role, but his loss was sudden and unexpected."

Justina nodded. "I see. Will you be seeking someone? I know of a man. He's well- connected, respectable, and honest. I could send him your way if you'd like."

Feeling at sea, it was Langdon's touch on her hand that settled the sudden flutter of concern. "Mr. Elgin was a naval man. Justina knows many men able to assist you. Perhaps you might send word to this person that he may call upon my wife later in the week if that suits you, Isabelle?"

Nodding, Isabelle made a mental note to talk to Langdon about his intervention later. For now, she'd keep her counsel.

"So, Mrs. Elgin, you intend to return to England. Do you have family there?"

Justina smiled. "I have children at school. I am returning closer to them and hope to open a small boarding house. I like people and bustle."

The words warmed Isabelle. Here wasn't a woman content to live quietly and eke out her existence but a woman who went after what she wanted. Perhaps she didn't pose a threat...

"Thanks to Langdon's assistance, I am able to do so," Justina added.

Isabelle stilled, her glance shooting to Langdon who'd excused himself from the room, but he stopped in the doorway and turned back.

"It's what friends do, Justina." He left, and Isabelle waited quietly, unsure what to do or say now.

"We were close once, Mrs. Deveraux, but have no doubts. He's got eyes for none but you. I have no designs upon him. He's a good and honest man, and I'm so lucky to call him a friend."

What did a woman do when told these things by a stranger? Particularly one she was sure had been intimate with her husband?

"I... Thank you, Mrs. Elgin."

"Justina," the woman urged as she gathered up the dishes.

"Justina then. I'm Isabelle."

Langdon returned, took in the plateau, and kept his silence as Justina bustled about clearing the remains of their meal. When she returned, Langdon held out a hand. "Many thanks, Justina, but we should leave now."

The woman smiled. "Farewell, Langdon. Isabelle."

They left the house, arms entwined. "You talked?"

Isabelle smiled. "She was a paramour of yours, yet I think I like her."

He gave her a sideways glance and a short nod. "I wouldn't have taken you there, but the situation was—"

"Pressing?" She smiled, but it died away as they moved swiftly in the direction of the house. "What do we do now?"

His hand clenched on hers. "We find Tang, and we make him talk."

"Will he tell you what you want to know?" It seemed far too easy to get Tang and interrogate him.

"No. We need leverage. I need to ask Mei and Jin Yun about his enterprises and how we can pin him for the opium importation. But we have one more iron for the fire. The Triad is fractured. The crone who brought me to you, she wants Tang removed from the leadership of the Triad and her husband installed in his place. I don't know how many others are wishful of the same outcome, but so long as they aren't importing opium or feeding the Russians information, the local constabulary can deal with them."

"But the girls," Isabelle implored.

"There is always an underbelly, Isabelle. We do what we can. At least this way the constables know who is running it and we have another bolt hole listed."

The sun rose in the sky, and Isabelle's head started to throb, but they continued walking, keeping to side alleys and laneways where possible. The echo of the cobbles beneath their feet the only sound now. Isabelle wondered if Langdon knew just how weary she was. His grip on her though remained a welcome pressure.

She'd never been so thankful when the view of the house rose. Before they could even reach for the door, it was thrust open, and Mrs. Hargraves bustled them inside.

Chapter Eighteen

THE PACING DIDN'T SOLVE anything, Langdon told himself, yet he found himself unable to do anything else. How would they trap Tang?

Mrs. Hargraves caught his attention. "Stubens is here, sir."

He stopped. "Send him in then."

She moved from sight just as Stubens entered the room. "Sir, I'm pleased you've got Mrs. Deveraux back. I've got men crawling the streets looking for signs of Tang Bao as you requested in your note. He's gone to ground, but I did receive some intelligence from Jin Yun. He's got a den where he keeps the opium near the hut, and with lookouts, that's probably how he worked out when you took the females. She—Jin Yun, I mean—has given me instructions on how to get there, and I'm putting a team together."

"When?" demanded Langdon.

"Tonight. But sir, you should stay here. Tang's men will be watching for you, and that might tip off a runner. We can't afford to lose this thread now. There's too much invested."

Langdon didn't like hearing that at all, yet he considered Stubens's words. This was the first real thread they'd had in four days since he'd returned to the house with Isabelle.

"Fine," he groused. "Once you have him in custody though, I want my time with him."

Stubens took one look at him then gave a silent nod. Langdon had made his stance on Tang clear. He would pay for what he'd done to Isabelle. Even if that had to come secondary to the other investigations.

"How's Mrs. Deveraux faring?" Stubens enquired, and Langdon frowned.

"Better than can be expected. She's meeting with a man this morning who might replace Staindhouse."

The man sniffed.

"Justina Elgin sent him."

Stubens's eyes slid into a high quirk. "Mrs. Elgin sent him. Your wife knows..."

Langdon rubbed his brow. "She does."

"Ahhh." Stubens shuffled his feet and waited in silence.

A rap on the door warned him Isabelle was about to enter. She slid inside, her hair glowing once more; only the dark rings beneath her eyes gave a hint to the ordeal she'd faced earlier in the week.

"Mr. Stubens. It's wonderful to see you again." She settled into the seat nearest Langdon.

"He's hoping to detain Tang tonight," Langdon informed Isabelle.

She opened her mouth, eyes wide, then closed her mouth once more.

"I'll remain here until Stubens sends word. He believes we are still under surveillance from Tang's men."

"Of course," she answered, but lines now bracketed her mouth.

She wasn't coping well with being watched by the man who'd held her prisoner, and she demanded answers just as Langdon did. It wasn't so much she feared he'd catch her again; Langdon had brought in men to protect the household. It was more that she'd been unable to visit the warehouse, and it curtailed her search for new and exotic products for Forster Shipping—a role she took seriously.

"Sir, Mrs. Deveraux, if you'll excuse me. I'll be getting the men ready as we'll move out immediately." Stubens beat a hasty retreat.

Langdon peered down at Isabelle. "How did your meeting with Faveaux unfold?"

She shook her head as if clearing some kind of haze. "Very well. He seems to know most of the warehouse tasks I'd expect him to undertake. Has connections to the suppliers, and made some suggestions for new lines. I'll check his references, but I feel he will be exactly what we require."

Langdon breathed a sigh of relief. This was the woman he'd fallen in love will. Assured and confident in her knowledge of her business.

"So, you'll hire him?"

"I believe so. He's also had experience dealing with the Triad and knows their ways. He's aware of how to avoid tangling with them. That did assist with my decision making too."

"Your plans for the rest of the day?" He settled into the seat opposite her, and she frowned.

"I should be busy. If it weren't for all the other interruptions, I'd likely be trying to make new connections with suppliers. But for now, I feel it best to remain here. I have the latest *La Belle Assemblée* to peruse." Her mouth pursed into a moue, and it delighted him. It was the first real flash of defiance or frustration she'd shown in days.

"Do you believe it will engage your attention?" He leaned forward, adding a hint of mischief to his words, and she smiled, her eyes glinting in the filtered sunlight.

"Perhaps. Maybe not." Isabelle stood and extended a hand. "What do you have in mind?"

"A walk in the greenhouse, then we'll see where it takes us."

She grasped his hand, and the warmth of her skin settled the nerves he'd barely realized afflicted him. They'd walked around on eggshells since her abduction. Each night he'd held her and wished he could do more. But he'd been there through her nightmares.

Held her in the dark nights when she'd sobbed out her fears. Every convulsive movement had driven a spike of rage into his brain, and the constant refrain in his mind said Tang would pay.

Langdon watched the tight way she'd held herself during the day and ensured she'd been cosseted and protected when the memories flashed her back to the moment she'd become aware. To the suppressed fury that speared his veins, and all because of Tang. He knew it would take time for Isabelle to come to terms with the memory of being shackled to the wall and stripped of her humanity.

The heat of the sun warmed him as he calmed the wave of violence that threatened to overwhelm him. "You are feeling improved?"

She faltered, then turned. "A little. As much as I try to forget what happened, the knowledge is always with me. Now I know how the women must have felt, ripped away from their families. Pressed into the life they didn't ask for or want. It's demeaning, Langdon."

They walked a little further, and he held open the greenhouse for her.

"I'd like to do more. When we return to England," she said. "These women deserve somewhere they can heal and be cared for until such time as they can train in a trade. I want to purchase a building, hire staff, and give them those opportunities. I've written to Aeddan already and asked if he could find a suitable building and staff. I sent it out yesterday aboard the East India vessel. I don't wish to bother Elspeth at this time, but when the next ship comes, I intend to send the women on it. The *Golden Chalice* arrives soon, then following that, the

Zephyr. I can send them directly to London. If he can arrange what I've requested by the time they arrive, Forster Shipping will sponsor the organization."

Langdon didn't know how he felt, knowing his wife had made so many arrangements without even mentioning this to him. "You weren't going to tell me?"

Isabelle whirled and turned to face him. "Forster Shipping is not you and I, Langdon. I'm used to making my own decisions." She thrust her hands up to make the point. "I am telling you now, so you're aware before it takes place, but I firmly stand by my decision. These women deserve more, and I'll do for them what should be done, to make things as right as possible."

Her cheeks glowed with fire, and her eyes sparkled, and it reminded him that she was indeed a woman of strength. She didn't need his permission or assistance. Perhaps that understanding did cost him a little, but he'd put aside his pettiness for this woman.

Not for the first time, he wondered if Aeddan had experienced even a small amount of frustration and concern for Elspeth, and if so, how he'd dealt with it. Strong women and strong men naturally must brush up against each other from time to time, but was it always like this? Scouring?

He dragged her close. "I won't ask you not to. Perhaps, in the future, some forward intelligence would be welcome," he whispered against her hair. She sagged, and he wondered if she'd expected him to remonstrate and argue with her.

"Thank you. I know I'm not like other women. I make decisions, and I'm used to everyone accepting them. I need to change some."

He grunted, and she laughed. "Perhaps a little. Not too much."

They spent time admiring the greenery, and she plucked an orange from a tree, the fruit out of season, making it a treasure in the winter months.

She pulled away. "Maybe we should eat?"

He wondered if she meant breaking a different, more carnal kind of breaking of their fast as they entered the house once more, having made their way in quick silence from the greenhouse.

They'd only stepped inside when a red-faced Mrs. Hargraves called. "Major? There's a runner here."

The woman thrust a note into his hands, and he broke the seal, scanned the message, then turned to Isabelle, who waited anxiously by his side. "I have to go." And in truth, he was regretful that he must leave now.

She nodded her understanding, and he headed for the door, aware this was their chance to break the back of the opium importation on one small branch.

Even as his fingers curled over the handle, he turned back, swept Isabelle into his arms, and kissed her. It was hard and rough. "I'll be back as soon as I can."

"I'll wait for you," she whispered.

"No. I'll likely be late. Sleep, and if it's not too late, I'll come to you." Then he left, his footsteps loud on the flagged floor.

Chapter Nineteen

ISABELLE FRETTED. The hours passed as she waited for Langdon.

"What can be taking so long?" Supper came and went. Her tea was drunk in silence, and the light meal only toyed with.

At midnight, she rose, gathered up the candle, and ascended the stairs in silence, having sent the staff to bed. The light meal she'd had placed in Langdon's room in case he required food when he finally came home.

Even as she settled into the bed, her gaze settled on her journal and she scooped it up, re- reading her final entry, written just before they entered the harbor.

Now she took up her pen and considered just how much had occurred since she'd last penned something.

"How do I begin?" she wondered aloud and started by penning the date.

So much has changed in a very little time. I have met and
married Langdon Deveraux, and honestly, I have reached heights
of pleasure and such lows of despair.
Elspeth and Aeddan left sometime ago, returning to England

with news of Elspeth's expectation, and Aeddan felt keenly the need to see his father, whom he'd heard was in ill health.

For myself, Shanghai has been a place of wonder.

The country, or as much as I've had the opportunity to see, is beautiful, and most of the people are welcoming. I do find myself constrained in the concession due to the vagaries of Langdon's role. There are times I find it restrictive, but he seeks so hard to ensure I enjoy a full recompense!

The society is not as full as I enjoyed in India, and I am now beginning to long for home. We have spoken at some length about settling once we return to England, and this morning, I felt the first stirrings of homesickness. Not so much for my childhood home, but for a society I understand.

My secret is not yet confirmed, but truly while I do not wish to curb Langdon's ability to fulfill his role, I now believe we will need to return to a settled existence sooner rather than later. Especially if my suspicions are correct.

There was so much to say, yet until Langdon had arrested the leader of the Triad, whom he felt lay at the heart of this opium importation ring, they'd be remaining here.

Isabelle took the time to carefully dry the pages before closing the journal and returning it to its place beside the chaise, then climbed into the bed, a book in hand.

She'd wait for Langdon, for as long as it took.

*L*angdon entered the house, bone-weary from the long hours interrogating Tang. He knew Isabelle would wish to see the outcome. There would be at least one more opportunity to talk to the man before he'd be hauled up before the municipal council, but all Langdon wanted was his bed and his woman.

He trudged up the stairs, a loud bong twice telling him it was two AM. Isabelle would be asleep, but he'd look in on her.

At the top of the stairs, he gazed at her door. Waking her wasn't an option, given he'd noted the exhaustion on her face in the last week. He opened the door, and she was perched on pillows, almost upright, eyes closed. In her lap was a book, and he smiled, thinking she'd likely attempted to stay up.

With quiet steps, he moved into the room and closed the door. Walking around the bed on silent feet, he meant only to retrieve the book then head for his room. He reached out, grasped the book, and she started upright, eyes wide and a scream building in her throat. He noted the terror and cursed himself even as he settled on the edge of the bed.

"I'm here, *ma belle*." He kept his voice low and calming, aware she needed to be soothed in the moment of fright.

"Langdon," she husked. "What time is it?"

"Late or early." He caressed her cheek. "You should be sleeping, *ma coeur*."

"I was waiting for you."

Isabelle's words filled him with pleasure. "I know. Now you should go back to sleep."

He leaned in and kissed her lips lightly. The chaste touch threatened to explode into a wild conflagration, but he tugged away. He rose, planning to sleep alone for the first time since they'd wed, to allow her a proper night's sleep.

"Where are you going?"

"To my room. You need sleep, *ma belle*."

"No. I sleep better with you. Don't leave me."

He frowned. Was she still that worried by the attack? If that were so, he would remain.

"I have something I wish to discuss with you." Isabelle bit her lip, color now high in her cheeks as she turned away.

Her actions intrigued him. "What?"

She shook her head, golden tresses whipping around her face, and she patted the space beside her. "Please?"

On a sigh, he began disrobing, watching her the entire time as she followed his moves, her gaze eager. The color of her eyes deepened to a midnight tone, and he wondered, not for the first time, how this had happened? How had he fallen in love with his wife? A woman who sparked him as clearly as he did her? Indeed, it was a marvel.

Langdon climbed into the bed beside her. Isabelle sighed, snuggled in, and he felt the slide of her gown against his skin. "You could remove this," he whispered, fingering the soft material.

"I could. Would you assist me?"

He caught the sounds of devilry in her words and grinned. Sleep would come later. He found the bottom edge of the gown in his grasp and slid it up so it pooled at her waist. She'd already unfastened the buttons at her chest, and with a couple of quick moves, he had the gown off. It sailed over her head and flew toward the end of the bed.

He pulled her into his arms, the softness of her skin rubbing against his flesh.

"I wanted to tell you something, Langdon." Her breath skittered over his chest.

"You can tell me anything, *ma belle*."

He felt her shake in his arms and waited in silence. "I'm... I believe I'm increasing." Her fingertips slid over his chest as the words pealed loudly in his ears. "Increasing? Expecting?"

Her gaze found his. "I believe so."

He crushed her closer then released her. What if he did her an injury? "You're sure?"

A crest of red filled her cheeks. "Not totally, but I believe I may be."

He nodded. "I should sleep in the other room then." He made to rise from the bed, but her hand stopped him.

"Why?" The word was full of surprise. "You won't hurt me."

He couldn't help the startled glance. "You're reading my mind."

She laughed now as if the pressure she'd been laboring under had washed away. "You truly have much to learn, husband."

"How soon will we know? Be able to be assured?" Now that the seed was planted in his mind, he could almost see a child, golden-haired with bright blue eyes.

"I'm of the opinion there isn't much doubt, husband. I've been unwell for over a week, and so very tired—in fact, exhausted. My monthly hasn't been since we were wed."

Langdon slid his hand over her abdomen. "Then we'll make plans to return to England."

"But Tang?"

He smiled. "He's in custody. But for now, let us sleep, *ma belle*. Tomorrow we'll talk, but for tonight I'm content to hold you."

Isabelle snuggled down into his arms. "Then all is well."

Chapter Twenty

ISABELLE FOLLOWED LANGDON'S INSTRUCTIONS. She wore a dark unadorned gown and fastened her hair high and pulled on a simple hat. Langdon had filled her in with the interrogation from the night before. Tang's men had sung like canaries, according to her husband. They feared the sentence that would befall them otherwise, and deals had been taken to ensure they'd told all.

Of course, even Isabelle knew that although this prostitution ring was broken, another would quickly spring up. There were always those who'd step in and take up the perfidious trade. Today was about gaining a name within the government. The person who'd traded in secrets to the detriment of the English government.

"Stay in the background," Langdon muttered as they slipped through the door, his fingers releasing hers, and she took a seat beside a constable. She'd be out of sight as long as she remained quiet.

She peered into the gloom and picked out Tang Bao easily as he was led into the tiny cell room, his face tight with fury.

"You'll release me now," the Chinese man growled as the rest of the interrogation party settled into their chairs beyond the metal grates separating the prisoner from those who'd assembled to interrogate him.

Langdon had already informed Isabelle that he'd named the person on the wharf acting as the go-between for the information trafficking. The offence, Langdon had assured her, that would see the man swing.

Now they wanted to find out who on her payroll was arranging the opium deliveries. They also needed to understand how that dovetailed with information trafficking. A tricky matter because the government did not wish to appear to be involved in stopping the trade, even though it was precisely what they intended to do.

"Tang Bao, we have already amassed a body of evidence highlighting that you've broken a range of laws, and it will be taken before a judge at a date to be determined. However, we also have intelligence that you've been acting as a go-between for the purposes of importing opium— a restricted substance —and using it to exert influence, to feed addiction and to enslave women for the express purposes of prostitution. Further, you abducted Mrs. Deveraux and demanded all investigations cease for her safe return." Stubens spoke clearly, facing the man directly while

Langdon sat stiffly at Stubens's side.

"We are prepared to make a deal, should you hand over the name of your contacts in the opium smuggling ring," added Langdon.

Tang Bao laughed. "You cannot make a deal. Only your government can do that." Langdon retrieved the message he'd carried from government house in his breast pocket and handed it to Stubens who led the interrogation.

"See this Tang?" Stubens held up the letter, ensuring Tang could see the crest emblazoned on the sheet of paper. "This is from government house. The consul himself penned it. It gives me the authority to handle these negotiations as I see fit. Major Deveraux himself met with him and obtained it."

Tang bared his teeth. "I should have killed the slut when—"

One of the constables had to hold Langdon down, and Isabelle could read the fury in every taut muscle of Langdon's body. It took a lot to keep her quietly sitting in the background too, but she'd promised Langdon she'd wait quietly no matter what was uttered.

Tang laughed. "You let a woman direct your actions. It makes you weak. They are only for our comfort."

Stubens cleared his throat. "So, you wish not to cooperate?"

Tang snarled.

"We know you had a man on the wharf. We know he was offloading crates and using Forster Shipping as a blind. He is now in our custody. The ceramic containers were filled with opium, and when Staindhouse got too close, you ordered his murder, we know all about that. You heard Deveraux was leading the investigation. It's just a shame you didn't know Deveraux was working for our government. He'd been placed in the municipal council to find out who and how the importation was taking place. His first hint was Staindhouse's murder. Dear me, very sloppy work that was too. The ginger jar we could trace back to your people along with your 'negotiations' with Staindhouse. He'd told both his wife and Mrs. Deveraux about them."

Tang grunted, curling his fingers. As Isabelle watched Stubens build the prosecution's case, she wondered how much of the information he was using Langdon had put together. If she didn't miss her mark, the majority of his efforts built the framework of the case.

Tang Bao rose and curled his hands around the metal grates. "I did arrange the opium. Inside the government, there is a man, Phillip Northcote. He arranged it all. He's the one you should arrest."

Isabelle knew that name. He was the contact, according to

Aeddan, that carried the government pouches the captains sent and received on behalf of the parliament. Her hand flew to her mouth, and she must have squeaked because Tang Bao saw or heard her in the dimness.

"So, he brought you along? The little woman who cries for her husband. I should have— "

This time no one could hold Langdon. He surged up and hit the man in the mouth through the metal uprights.

Tang Bao reared back, blood streaming, his eyes slits of murder. "You are dead," he snarled, and Stubens called for the constable.

Men streamed into the holding cell, grabbing Tang Bao and hauling him back. The squeak of metal filling the air as Tang screamed his threats.

Langdon turned and strode to Isabelle where she waited, his knuckles split and bloody. He extended his hand, and she took it.

Stubens bellowed for quiet, and finally, it came as Langdon held her hand. "We have the information we require, Stubens. Attend to the rest."

"Tang Bao, you will be charged with abduction, the carrying out of prostitution, the importation of opium, and finally, also with conspiring against His Majesty's government. You will be returned to your cell, and as soon as a judge can be apprised of the brief, you will be judged."

Tang snarled, and Langdon whirled. "Tang, you should be aware, more than one of these charges, should they be substantiated, will culminate in the sentence of death. You may think me weak, but while you face your maker, I will be far from here. Living my life. Enjoying it."

With that, he turned and ushered Isabelle from the room. Once they had stepped out of the interrogation area Isabelle took the first deep breath she'd taken since they'd stepped inside. "That room reeks," she muttered, and Langdon laughed.

"That's all you have to offer?" Langdon looked so insulted that she stifled any further laughter that rose.

"Well, no. You were my hero?" She smiled, hoping it would break through the icy barrier of frigid rage he'd cloaked himself in.

His gaze narrowed. "Isabelle?"

"Whatever I have to say, I can't and won't do here, Langdon. Let's go home. We have plans to make and things to discuss." She took his arm, and they walked toward the exit, and as they stepped into the sunshine, a ray of sunlight almost blinded her.

He urged her into the carriage that was waiting at the bottom of the steps, and they traveled home.

*L*angdon waited in his library. There were plans to make, as Isabelle had pointed out when they'd left the offices of the constabulary. Things to consider, and they'd need to arrange passage to England forthwith. His child would be born in their home, especially given if it was a boy, he would eventually be the heir of the Earl of Ravenhelm when his grandfather and father passed on.

The door opened, and Stubens settled opposite him. "I've passed on the information to government house. They'll send a packet to the prime minister. It'll go via the admiralty to ensure the security of the information."

"So my job here is done." Langdon stretched back in his seat, pinning the man opposite with a piercing look. "You've done an exceptional job, Stubens."

Stubens blinked slowly. "Thank you, sir, or should I say Your Lordship?"

Now it was Langdon's turn to feel surprised. "You knew?"

"It's my job to find out who everyone is. I've known since you arrived but kept my counsel."

Landon laughed. "Of course you did. An excellent job you did too."

The rap of knuckles echoed, and Isabelle strode into the library. "Mr. Stubens. It's a pleasure to see you again under happier circumstances."

"Your Ladyship. It's a pleasure to see you as well."

Isabelle's glance settled on Langdon, and he read the question in her eyes. "He worked it out by himself. Now, if you'd excuse us, Stubens, we have some plans to make."

The man shook his hand. "Well, I'll be making my farewells then. I'm to be sent to India."

"You'll enjoy it there, Stubens. Sunshine, good food, and robust society," added Isabelle, and the man nodded.

When he'd left, Isabelle settled into the seat he'd vacated. "I've received news the *Zephyr* will be here in just over a week. She's made excellent time. If you're comfortable, we could travel back to England aboard her. She's only stopping for re-provisioning."

Langdon gazed at her, questioning the intent of her comment. "What about seeking new items to import?"

Isabelle plucked at her gown. "I've concluded that I should allow those better connected to do that. I've given some directions to Faveaux concerning some furnishings I desire to see imported, but to be honest, I want to go home, Langdon."

"Then home we'll go. We'll need to stop in London. I intend to hand in my commission."

She gazed at him. "I thought you already had."

Langdon shook his head. "No. I've allowed people to think that as it suited us all, especially the government, but the time has come to take my place in society. To learn about my family and to assume my role in the family. After all, the next generation will be here soon enough, and I intend to be home every night to enjoy them."

"I'm not giving up Forster Shipping," she said, and he shook his head.

"I've never asked that of you, though you may take some time perhaps for our child."

"And any that come after it," Isabelle added. "I've spoken with Mei. She and Fuchs will begin preparing our trunks. Mrs. Hargraves has been informed, and while she's told me she's sad to see our departure, she wishes us well."

"Organizing me already?"

"Just a little," Isabelle laughed and rose up, circling the desk to him. He reached for her, and she settled against his chest.

Epilogue

ISABELLE WAITED IN THE CARRIAGE, already feeling far too cumbersome and large to join Langdon within the building where he'd officially deliver the letter declaring his intention to surrender his commission. Her hand rested on the swell of her belly—the fluttering within having long ago given into jabs and wriggles.

The conveyance rocked as Langdon climbed back in, and he dragged her close. "Well, wife, I believe that task is now complete and we're ready to make our journey home."

"John Coachman informs me that Mei and Fuchs were sent on and will have rooms ready for use at the inn, only the most necessary items are in trunks, and the horses are fresh. And you're sure your parents have no issues with us going straight to the house?"

Langdon cupped her cheek, his thumb rubbing over her lips. "No. They understand that we don't wish to prolong the trip."

"I do look forward to meeting them, and to be honest, after months of travel, the thought of a home does indeed fill me with pleasure."

The *Zephyr* had traveled quickly, with good winds and fair currents, but it was still a long way to travel from Shanghai to London. They'd taken up residence in a hotel for the last several weeks while Langdon had settled his affairs in town and made arrangements to travel to their home on the coast of Suffolk, with the blessing of his parents.

"When we reach Lowestoft you can make the arrangements you feel necessary to move Forster Shipping to there." Langdon gathered her close. "Have you heard from Elspeth and Aeddan?"

Isabelle bit her lip. "No, I didn't receive any news before I quit the hotel. Only that he felt she was in labor, as you know."

Langdon placed his hands over her now ripe belly. "Soon they will be awaiting news of our child, Isabelle."

She slid her hand over his. "Yes. I never thought this would happen. I wrote in my journal just before I reached Shanghai that I doubted I'd ever feel this attachment, then there you were, Langdon, and my world changed."

Isabelle looked out on the road, realizing that the rocking of the carriage had heralded their leaving London.

"I wonder," she whispered and pulled the carriage curtains closed. "In Shanghai, late one night, you told me about carriages. Perhaps now is as good a time as any?"

His gaze sharpened. His mouth widened into a grin as interest rose between them, the scent of hunger filling the air. "Are you sure you're able?"

Isabelle gave a moue. "I'm expecting, not dying, Langdon."

He laughed and hauled her close. "Then we begin." He reached for her jacket and slipped the buttons free as his lips found hers.

The passion between them exploded, and when she pulled away, it was to whisper, "Oh, Langdon."

**I hope you've enjoyed *Miss Isabelle's Craving*.
To see more Imogene Nix books, just turn the page!**

Inheritance Of The Blood by Imogene Nix

In the darkness evil waits…

As a young bride Kira was whisked away from everything and everyone she knew, including her new husband and became Christina, an operative of the Displaced Persons Unit.

As the danger grows she sees an opportunity to save her husband Vasya and sister Serina. But nothing is the same. Serina is grown up——married and pregnant.

Vasya too is older and darkly forbidding. Trusting Christina doesn't come easily until a catastrophic event takes place. Now, knowing the truth everything he thought he knew is changed. But at a very high cost.

The four must work together to defeat the Demon, Zuor and the stakes are higher than they imagined and all could be lost.

The burning at the back of her neck warned she was being watched. A quick glance didn't clarify it. Instead, she turned around in time to see her mother's face, pale. "Mama?"

She took a step forward, but her grandfather snatched her wrist.

The grip was painful, and Kira stilled. "Let your parents talk."

She didn't know what the topic of conversation was, but it couldn't be good.

The dappled sunlight seemed cooler than before.

Her father crooked his forefinger at her grandfather while they stood there. For a moment she wished Vasya had come with them, but he had to work. Just the thought of her new husband warmed Kira.

She only had a few minutes to contemplate her newly defined status as a married woman, when her grandfather pulled at her hand. "Come with me." He tugged and, confused, Kira allowed herself to be towed away.

A glance at her parents' faces stole any feeling of well-being. "Grandfather?"

"Shh, my love. You must go." His grip was implacable and his face stern, but he shivered.

"What are you doing? Where are you taking me, Grandfather?"

They moved rapidly through the village they'd visited to sell their wares just that morning, and for the first time since they'd arrived in the market place she felt fear. What was wrong? Was it something to do with Vasya?

"You are in danger. We must send you away." The words confused her further. Send her away? Danger?

"Where is Vasya?" She stumbled over a stone, but he kept tugging her onwards.

With a quick glance around, he hauled her into a dirty laneway between the buildings. Kira gasped, trying to drag air into her starving lungs. "There's no time. We must get you away."

A nondescript shopfront lay ahead, and he pushed on the door. It rattled and opened with a loud groan. "Andre? Andre, are you here?"

An older man shuffled into the room, bent nearly double from the weight of the load on his back. "Marat? What do you want?"

"My granddaughter. They are coming for her and us. Get her away. Take her now, while you can."

The man's face clouded over. "Are you sure?"

"Grandfather, where is Vasya?" Fright had the blood in her veins pounding.

"Hush, my precious. Andre will see you well." He turned. "Whatever it takes, Andre. Take her now." With surprising speed, her grandfather whirled and was gone.

The man, Andre, eyed her. "Come this way, child. There is no time to be lost."

Eleven years later

The tattoo of her heart and cry of terror woke her, as they usually did. Once again, as she had since that rapid flight from those who sought her, she found herself in a lonely bed. Hundreds of miles away from everything she'd dreamed of, in a house she'd built for them to share. As always, it left her wishing that Vasya had fled with her.

Instead, here she was, exiled without her husband. With a sob, she rolled over and let the tears fall.

Available from Beachwalk Press
books2read.com/IOTB

Direct Autographed Copy
http://bit.ly/2w6g4K6

When Cupid—otherwise known as Diocail— is banished from his home on a remote Scottish Island, he's set a series of tasks by the great god Lugh, who also happens to be his father.

In **Blame The Wine**, he must bring two lovers together... BBW Cara and James, the man she's lusted over from afar who happens to be a super geek and head Veha Industries.

In **A Stranger's Embrace**, Diocail is driven to help an emotionally fragile Jane and Davis, a famous author. The task is more complicated, with the existence of Carstairs her could-be ex-husband and teenage daughter, Frannie.

In **Revenge on Cupid**, Diocail must take the ultimate chance and find his own happily ever after with Simone. Sometimes the past gets in the way and HEA's don't come cheap though.

The dusty, dingy little diner was full, even with its current state of cleanliness—or lack thereof. People from the surrounding offices didn't care about anything except the incredible, well-prepared food at a reasonable cost. They flooded in, like waves to the shore. As one tide left, another swept in.

"Honestly, Simone. I'm going to try getting his attention one more time. If that doesn't work, I'm out of there. I mean, how long can I keep trying?" Cara picked at the caramel tart she hadn't been able to resist with the cheap metal fork and flicked the blob of fresh cream that sat on top to the side of the plate.

"You've said that tons of times before. Besides, what are you going to do to get his attention? Hmm? Walk naked through the typing pool?" Simone bobbed the straw in her smoothie as she eyed her friend with a frown. "It's been what? Eighteen months since you saw him, and you've mooned over him from a distance ever since you met him. You need to move on, Cara. That is, unless there's something you haven't shared?"

The query was arch. Cara shivered even as she shook her head. "No."

Simone quirked an eyebrow, obviously unconvinced with the answer. Cara let out a deep sigh 1of frustration. "There's a position...it's only temporary, for a PA reporting directly to him." She speared a forkful of tart, chewed quickly and swallowed, before continuing. "In his office, full-time for the period of the engagement. I saw the memo yesterday. I mean, I have the skills, right? I can type, answer phones, make coffee, file, greet people. What's more, I can probably do it better than all those size eights in the typing pool that Ms. Jackman seems to prefer." She nodded thoughtfully. "All I have to do is get past the ogre in Human Resources."

Simone stared at her, disbelief clear on her face. "Girl, I so remember that woman. If you think you can get past her, you're doing better than I ever did. That's why I left Veha Industries, remember? Maybe it's time to haul out your resumé and consider some other options. Look for something better." Simone shook her head and billows of her crimson hair swirled through the still air.

Cara understood Simone only had her best interests at heart. But this time she knew the outcome would be different. Hell, she could feel it in the air. The tingle of expectation.

"Cara, the HR ogre will hang you out for breakfast before she offers you anything like a position in that office. Remember her mantra? Good looks and good work make for a positive workplace!"

Simone didn't sugar-coat anything. It was another great reason for their long- term friendship. Honesty. But Cara didn't want to hear the truth in the statement. Even if it was exactly as her friend said.

Cara nodded quickly. "Yeah, I know, but if I don't try, then I won't know how close I can get to him, right? And the only way to catch his attention is to get past *her* and see him in person." Cara quaked a little at the information she needed to share. The favor she needed to ask. "Anyway, I tidied up my resumé and dropped the application into a memo envelope yesterday, so it's too late to back out now. I mean, fortune favors the brave. Doesn't it? If I don't snag an interview, I'm going to visit the career advisor across the street and register with them." She shrugged. "I'll look for temp work until something more long-term shows up. I can see what they have on offer and well...who knows? Maybe a job with the right boss is just waiting for me. But I'd rather this worked out, to be honest." Her voice trailed off into a whisper. "I really wish he would notice me."

Simone took a long slurp of her banana drink, and Cara noticed her questioning gaze even as she squirmed. Finally, Simone nodded. "It's your funeral. So anyway, you'd better show me this memo if you want me to be a referee for you. I'm guessing that's what you need, right? I'll have to know what I'm supposed to say about you before they ring."

Cara smiled. "Thanks, Simone. I knew I could count on you." She slipped a piece of paper out of her handbag and handed it over. "Sorry it's a bit creased. It was in the bottom of my bag, I stashed it so none of the others from the pool would see. You know how it is."

Available from Love Books Publishing
books2read.com/CelticCupid

Direct Autographed Copy
http://bit.ly/2vs7wtS

BioCybe by Imogene Nix

Can a cyber-enhanced warrior and a ship's captain find love together?

Levia Endrado never wanted to be a warrior, but at seventeen she was deemed suitable for battle. After intense training and multiple enhancements, which gave her superior strength and healing ability, she was sent off to defeat the enemy—a killing machine with a mission.

When the war was over, she had to find a new life. At twenty-seven she's a washed-up veteran without a future. Or she was, until she met Sandon Daria.

Serving as a pilot aboard Sandon's spaceship the *Golden Echo* makes Levia long for a different and gentler life. But old hurts and even older enemies aren't so easily forgotten. Particularly when they come back for her.

Sandon is determined to show Levia that she's more than just a BioCybe…she's the woman who completes him. Getting close is just the first step, keeping her alive is an even bigger challenge, but one he's willing to take because the prize is their combined future.

Levia scanned the long line of other hopefuls entering the chamber. The large building in the center of town was cold, and she dragged her wrap around her body, even as she craned her head, looking to the high ceiling. She'd never before had an occasion to enter the testing complex, yet she'd seen the lines of teenagers every time they passed the building.

Once she'd asked her parents why the teens were lined up and her mother's face had shuttered. Her stepfather had just shaken his head and growled. They'd stopped her questions with a carefully uttered, "You'll know soon enough, Levia." The pain in her mother's eyes had been enough to shush her questions. For endless months afterward, her parents had traveled different routes to the educational facility she attended and Levia lost interest in the puzzle of that building.

Now, as she looked around, remembering that long ago spring day, it was her opportunity to find out. But she felt a surge of concern at what lay ahead. She likely wasn't the only one, given that there were probably two to three hundred seventeen-year-olds gathered in the one place. Ahead of her, she caught sight of a couple of girls, their arms linked together and wide smiles on their faces. Scanning the crowd, she became aware that, by far, a majority of those gathered displayed both fear and trepidation.

"All female subjects will enter through doors three, six, and seven. All male subjects will enter through gates four, eight, and ten." The speaker above her was loud, and she jumped before checking the numbers etched on the black metal sign over her head.

The massive doors beside her swung open, and now an uncertain silence reigned. Many of the youngsters hung back, clearly discomforted by whatever testing regime lay ahead. This was where they'd been told their futures would be determined.

"Oh gosh, I hope they only have an aptitude and psych eval. I don't think..." Levia turned to see the white face of the girl behind her. The girl had uttered what many must silently be thinking.

Levia dragged an unsteady breath in, her hand resting flat against the plane of her belly as she looked around. No one had entered yet. It was clear many were on the verge of taking the step, but still they hung back.

She straightened her shoulders. "I'm not afraid." It was always wiser to approach things head-on, she believed. When her biological father had died, she'd been one of the few to view his capsule before it was sent into the massive gray structure built to accommodate those who'd moved onto the next life realm.

Her legs shook as she wobbled toward the entrance. Beyond the doorway, she spied sealed cubicles and her heart stuttered. Why cubicles? Usually testing—med and psych—were in eval-units, hidden only by billowing white curtains. She glanced back, noting that others had taken the first step.

"Move along, subjects." Once again, the androgynous voice of the address system blared.

Of course, given it was her seventeenth anniversary of birth, she was technically considered an adult now.

She thought longingly of baby Rald and her half-sister, Elda, waiting at home for her to return, and the celebrations to be held that night. That made her smile. She would need to make them proud of her.

She entered a row and the tall Educational Specialist, the edu-specs as her peers laughingly called them, stopped her. "Present your credentials to the scanner."

She'd done this many times since the tiny implant had been slipped below the dermal layer of her skin at birth. The small unit in her wrist heated as her details were checked.

"Enter the first cubicle, Levia Endrado, and follow the instructions to complete your assessment."

Thus dismissed, Levia moved to the first unit, laid her palm against the scanner, and the door slid open soundlessly.

"Welcome, Levia Endrado. Take your place in the eval-unit." The soft contralto of the voice echoed after the door closed silently behind her.

"What are you evaluating?" Her voice was breathy, and she peered around.

"Your skills—physical and psychological. Your emotional and medical status. Your educational attainment levels."

It was an answer that shed little insight into the many things she was hungry to know. "Why do all seventeen year olds—"

"Take a seat, Levia. Then we may begin your testing."

If she'd expected an answer, she was sadly mistaken, she considered sourly. She dropped into the seat, the soft leather-like surface molding to her body.

"Levia Endrado, you are required to remove all non-specified apparel."

She jolted in the chair. "It's cold."

"The temperature will be amended. Remove the non-specified apparel."

Her misgivings grew as she dragged off the light wrap she'd brought with her, and then threw it to the floor at the side of the unit.

"We will begin, Levia Endrado. At any time, should you experience any malfunctions of the unit, simply depress the red button." It glowed and she grimaced.

Levia reclined against the chair and waited for the testing to begin.

The first examination was based on her understanding of the political system, where she saw herself, and her knowledge of the rights and responsibilities accorded through citizenship of both her planet and the commonwealth.

The second test was mathematical and scientific proficiency. It felt like hours had passed by the time she'd finished, and she lay limp on the seat, exhausted.

"Levia Endrado, you may rise. The sanitary unit will emerge once you trigger the yellow button at the door. Should you require refreshment, press the blue button and a restorative will be made available."

"Can I leave?"

"Negative, Levia Endrado. Your needs will be catered for in this capsule."

"Why?" Her voice hitched and true fear rose for the first time. Why did they keep her in the alcove?

"All will be revealed at the end of the testing cycle."

Levia looked at the now empty screen before hurling a curse word. It was met with silence.

The urgent throb of her bladder reminded her that she needed to use the facilities, so, with

a sigh, she rose and clambered from the seat. After attending to the needs of her body, she walked around the unit, peering at the door, but it was obviously programmed remotely. She poked and prodded, but it made no difference. With a huff, she headed back to the chair.

The moment she'd settled in, the viewing screen shone

bright. "Welcome back, Levia. The next sequence will evaluate your psychological reflexes, then that will be followed up with the general knowledge portion of the evaluation."

"When can I leave?" It seemed better to ask bluntly, she told herself.

"Once the examination is completed. After the next set of evaluations, you will be subjected to the physical aspect."

"Then I can go home?"

"Levia Endrado, you will now complete the psychological test. This will be undertaken by one of the center's personal evaluators."

She frowned. Personal evaluators? She bit her lip, and the sting reminded her that this wasn't something to joke about. In her seventeen years, she'd only heard of personal evaluators being brought in once before, and that was when one of the girls at her academy had been in a serious accident. Both legs were amputated and her body's ability to keep her alive had been gravely compromised. Her peers had been informed that the girl had requested the assessment before she could request her support systems be disconnected.

"Levia Endrado, are you ready to recommence processing?" The emotionless voice echoed once more and she gulped.

"Yes."

Available from Beachwalk Press
http://www.beachwalkpress.com

Direct Autographed Books
http://bit.ly/BioCybe

Also by Imogene Nix

Warriors of the Elector

- Star of Ishtar
- Starline
- Starfire
- Star of the Fleet
- Starburst
- The Star of Eternity

The Star of Ishtar & Starline - Print

Starfire & Star of the Fleet - Print

Starburst & The Star of Eternity - Print

Blood Secrets (Re-releasing 2020)

- The Blood Bride
- The Illuminated Witch
- The Sorcerer's Touch

The Search Duology

- Miss Elspeth's Desire
- Miss Isabelle's Craving

Reunion Trilogy

- War's End
- The Assassin
- Executing Justice

The Reunion Trilogy in Paperback

Sex Love & Aliens

- Tangled Webs
- False Webs (Sex Love & Aliens Vol 1)
- Covert Webs (Sex Love & Aliens Vol 2)

21st Testing Protocol

- Cyborg: Redux
- Children Of A Greater Evil
- When Evil Came To Stay (Not Yet Released)
- Finis: The War To End All Wars (Not Yet Released)

Celtic Cupid Trilogy

- Blame The Wine
- A Stranger's Embrace
- Revenge On Cupid

The Celtic Cupid Trilogy in Paperback

Zombieology

- The Reset (2018 - Love At The End of The World)
- I Dream of Zombies (2019)
- The Six Million Dollar Zombie (Coming 2020)

Knights of Pleasure

- Silken Knights (Not Yet Released)

Single Titles

The Chocolate Affair (also in Print)

Falling In Love Again (Previously A Sapphire For Karina)

BioCybe (also in Print)

Hesparia's Tears (also in Print)

Tomorrow's Promise

A Bar In Paris (also in Print)

Inheritance Of The Blood (also in Print)

The Plan

Loving Memories (also in Print)

Hero of Heartbreak Hill (also in Print)

My One & Only (coming 2020)

Raspberry Dreams (Not Yet Released)

Non Fiction

Self Publishing: Absolute Beginners Guide (With Suzi Love)

Written as Ciara Cave

25 Curated Ways To Get Rid Of Telemarketers

Book Signings for Absolute Beginners

About the Author

Imogene is published in a range of romance genres including Paranormal, Science Fiction and Contemporary. She is mainly published in the UK and USA.

In 2010, Imogene Nix (the pen name not Imogene herself) was born. Imogene sat down and worked tirelessly for 3 months culminating in the book Starline, which became the first in a trilogy titled, "Warriors of the Elector." Since then she's had over 30 titles published and is now focusing on hybridising herself - with a mixture of traditionally published and self-published works.

In fact, she's taking control of many of her back catalogue books, which are slowly re-releasing as self-published titles.

Imogene is a member of a range of professional organisations world wide, and believes in the mantra of mentoring and paying it forward and is actively involved in mentorship (through NaNoWrimo and her vlog: In The Chair With Imogene Nix) and tutoring of new and upcoming authors.

In her spare time she loves to drink coffee, wine & eat chocolate and is parenting her spoiled dog and a ferocious cat along with her husband and 2 human daughters and looks forward to weekends away with her husband in their caravan "The Seven Year Hitch!" Do look forward to her caravan romance at some point!

To Contact Imogene
www.imogenenix.net
imogene@imogenenix.net

 facebook.com/ImogeneNix
twitter.com/ImogeneNix
instagram.com/ImogeneNix